"When you're away from me, I can't protect you."

Wayne took hold of Jessie's shoulders and continued a little desperately, "Do you think I don't know what's out there waiting for you? Drunks and loners. Honky-tonks filled with wannabe studs. Cheap motel rooms with no security."

"Wayne, I've been traveling for ten years. I know how to look after myself."

"I don't agree. When you're on stage, you invite men's fantasies. You're a danger to yourself."

"So either I give up the tour or I give up you?"

"Jessie, I love you. I want to take care of you."

"You have a dream of what you want. I don't fit it." Jessie picked up her guitar and took a moment to study Wayne.

Then, her hand on the doorknob, she said softly, "I love you. Goodbye."

Special thanks and acknowledgment to Cara West for her contribution to the Crystal Creek series.

Special thanks and acknowledgment to Sutton Press Inc. for its contribution to the concept for the Crystal Creek series.

ISBN 0-373-82521-8

GUITARS, CADILLACS

Guitars, Cadillacs

Cara West

Harlequin Books

TORONTO • NEW YORK • LONDON
AMSTERDAM • PARIS • SYDNEY • HAMBURG
STOCKHOLM • ATHENS • TOKYO • MILAN
MADRID • WARSAW • BUDAPEST • AUCKLAND

Dear Reader,

"Harlequin's new special series called Crystal Creek wonderfully evokes the hot days and steamy nights of a small Texas community... impossible to put down until the last page is turned."

—*Romantic Times*

If this is your first visit to Crystal Creek, come meet Sheriff Wayne Jackson—and the McKinneys, the Randolphs and the Joneses...just a few of the folks who live, love and ranch in the small Texas Hill Country community of Crystal Creek. And if you're returning for more of the linked stories you love, you won't be disappointed with the romances some of your favorite authors still have in store for you! Barbara Kaye, Margot Dalton, Bethany Campbell, Sharon Brondos, Kathy Clark and Cara West have created wonderful tales with a true Texas flavor and all the elements you've come to expect in your romance reading: compelling, contemporary characters caught in conflicts that reflect today's dilemmas.

In *Guitars, Cadillacs,* the sheriff finds himself spending a lot more time than usual at Zack's, drawn there by the mesmerizing Jessica Reynolds, an up-and-comer on the country music scene. He follows her to Austin, but knows for certain where he'll refuse to follow her—on tour. No way will he become a groupie for a celebrity! Besides, something is going down at Zack's, and Wayne wants to be where he can do what he does best—keep the law and order in Crystal Creek!

Next month, Wayne will have new problems to deal with, when things go awry at the Gibsons' Flying Horse Ranch. Manny Hernandez, Crystal Creek's veterinarian, finds himself enmeshed in something sinister at the Flying Horse, and it threatens to lose him the love and respect of Tracey Cotter, the numbers whiz behind the success of Cal McKinney's new boot shop venture. Watch for Kathy Clark's *Stand By Your Man* in December, wherever Harlequin Books are sold.

C'mon down to Crystal Creek—home of sultry Texas drawls, smooth Texas charm and tall, sexy Texans!

Marsha Zinberg
Coordinator, Crystal Creek

A Note from the Author

Austin has been called the Gateway to the Texas Hill Country, which is the setting for the Crystal Creek series. I have lived in Austin for over twenty years and vow I will never live anyplace else. When March arrives and tender green shoots soften the rocky grays and browns, when bluebonnets blossom to carpet the hillsides nestling up to the perennial cacti, when spring gentles the untamed Texas landscape, there is no place on earth more delightful to be.

Cara West

Cast of Characters

AT THE DOUBLE C RANCH

John Travis (J.T.) McKinney	Rancher, owner of the Double C, his family's ranch. A man who knows his own mind.
Cynthia Page McKinney	J.T.'s wife. An ex-Bostonian bank executive learning to do things the Texas way.
Tyler McKinney	J.T.'s eldest son, a graduate of Rice University. Now he wants to grow grapes in his daddy's pasture.
Cal McKinney	J.T.'s second son, an irresistible and irrepressible rodeo cowboy.
Serena Davis	The boot maker who turned Cal's head.
Lynn McKinney	J.T.'s only daughter. She bucks the trend by raising Thoroughbreds in quarter horse country.
Hank Travis	J.T.'s ancient grandfather. Old Hank has seen and done it all.
Ruth Holden	Californian vintner, daughter of Dan Holden, J.T.'s old army buddy. Ruth is visiting the Double C to help Tyler plan his vineyard.

AT ZACK'S PLACE

Zack Stone	Owner of Zack's—a true honky-tonk kicker palace.
Jessica Reynolds	A rising country and western star.
Wayne Jackson	The sheriff of Crystal Creek. He's keeping an eye on things.

AT THE LONGHORN

Dottie Jones	Owner of the Longhorn Motel and Coffee Shop.
Nora Jones	Dottie's son's ex-wife.
Bubba Gibson	A good old boy, owner of the Flying Horse Ranch.

AT THE HOLE IN THE WALL

Scott Harris	He's exchanged his pinstripes for chaps and a Stetson, to create his dream, the Hole in the Wall Dude Ranch.
Valerie Drayton	Scott's new wife and partner in the ranch.
Jeff Harris	Scott's brother. Once the Hole in the Wall puts a few bucks in his pocket, he's heading for his true love: the Texas oil fields.

CHAPTER ONE

SHE WAS FIRE—blazing fire—and shimmering darkness.

Wayne let out a ragged sigh as an overwhelming need pulsed through him. He sagged against the wall, hoping the dim lighting hid his body's reaction. Hoping his face remained impassive. Hoping he didn't look like he'd been kicked in the gut.

He'd seen her before—from a distance, that is. A bird of paradise set down in a nest of sparrows. A couple of times lately he'd noticed her at the café with Dottie. He understood Dottie and she were good friends. He'd also spotted her once in Zack's Bronco. Rumor had it those two were more than friendly.

Wayne had heard that her singing was as spectacular as her looks. But since he wasn't interested in singers, spectacular or otherwise, he hadn't bothered to find out for himself.

Maybe he'd known somewhere beyond consciousness that watching her perform might prove dangerous. That same sense of danger now urged him to run far and fast.

Instead, he stood stunned into stillness.

Under the spotlights, she literally shimmered. A red-beaded dress clung to her curves. Milk-white breasts spilled over her bodice. Flaming red hair tangled wantonly around her face. Every inch of her was an invitation. Hell, she was a sexual fantasy come to life.

But it wasn't so much her beauty that disturbed Wayne. After Michelle, after the NFL groupies, after four years of patrolling the Strip in Las Vegas, surface perfection left him unmoved.

It wasn't the sight of her that caused his pulse to hammer. It was hearing her, feeling her, absorbing her brilliance. Inside her was a passion that poured out with every song.

Her voice, when she spoke, brushed against him like velvet. When she sang, he heard laughter, hunger and tears. Her husky timbre was a siren call luring him closer.

Want me, she sang. *Need me. Take me. Love me.*

Wayne turned on his heel to walk out the door.

"Jessie's something else, isn't she, Sheriff?" Tiny, the bouncer, blocked the exit of Zack's Place.

Not trusting himself further, Wayne grunted a response.

Wild applause punctuated the end of a song.

Tiny shook his head musingly. "Jessie sure fires up an audience. Most of these guys wish they could get her into bed. They probably wouldn't last five minutes between the sheets with her. But I can't blame them for dreaming. Can you?"

Wayne didn't think it wise to answer Tiny's wistful question. Better to end the conversation. "Well, that's what she's selling—dreams and fantasies."

He tried to ease around Tiny, but Tiny didn't take the hint.

"You mean that body of hers?" he asked. "Maybe so. But Jessie's a lot more than boobs and bottom. I've caught every honky-tonk act from here to Amarillo. I know talent when I see it. And that little lady is headed for the big time, if someone doesn't eat her up and spit her out first."

"She looks like she can take care of herself," Wayne murmured.

"Don't let that glitz and glamour fool you, Sheriff. She's one of the nicest, most down-to-earth gals I know."

"I'm sure." Once again Wayne moved to step around the bouncer.

But Tiny was intent on his own agenda. "Listen, Sheriff, thanks for dropping by. I really appreciate it."

"No problem, Tiny. That's what I get paid for."

"I figured I could handle the ruckus," Tiny said. "But I told Tom, the bartender, to call you, in case they needed to cool off in jail."

"What happened exactly?"

"The usual. Two men trying to beat each other stupid. I was able to show them the error of their ways."

"Too much to drink?"

"And only one woman."

"What happened to the woman?"

"She threw beer on both of them and rushed out in tears."

Wayne grinned, relaxing a little, now that his back was to the stage. "That should have cooled them off."

"Good thing, too." Tiny swelled up to his considerable size. "I was fixin' to have to butt their heads together."

Wayne gave Tiny's shoulder a friendly slap. "Well, it looks like you have things in hand, so I'll take off."

"Oh, damn," Tiny muttered, glancing past Wayne.

Wayne turned to follow Tiny's look.

Jessica Reynolds had just finished her set. Her departure was greeted with boos and catcalls, but Wayne didn't spot anything foreshadowing a disturbance in the audience. Then he noticed Zack waiting for her at the bottom of the stairs.

Zack hugged her in apparent congratulation. She gave him back a wary smile. Then he groped her bare back and shoulder, sliding one hand below her waist to fondle her rear.

When she stepped away, he urged her closer, both his hands grabbing whatever they could find.

"Dammit," Tiny said. "He can't get it through his head she's not easy pickin's."

They watched as she twisted around and said something, all the while attempting to evade Zack's grasp. This time he jerked her against him and whispered in her ear.

They had become the focus of everyone's attention. The usual barroom noise had subsided to a hush.

"Now he's starting to play rough," Tiny said, his hands clenching in frustration.

Without another word, Wayne left the bouncer's side and threaded his way toward the stage.

THE FIRST HINT Jessie had of her rescuer was a steely voice cutting between them. A steely voice coming from a mountain of a man.

"Is something the matter?" the man asked.

Zack's expression stiffened. "This is private, Sheriff Jackson. Tiny took care of the drunks."

"It doesn't look very private to me."

Jackson glanced around the room full of ogling customers, giving Jessie time to do some staring of her own. Although she was tall, he towered over her a good eight inches, and she figured he weighed at least 230 pounds.

His sudden appearance should have given Zack warning. But Zack hadn't caught the significance of it.

"Come on, we'll go into my office." He grabbed Jessie by the wrist and pulled her toward a door.

"That should be private enough," Jackson said, arriving there first. As soon as the three were inside, he stepped in front of Zack and clamped a hand around his forearm. With a flick of his wrist, he loosened Zack's hold.

Jessie felt her mouth go slack at the effortless maneuver.

Zack stared down at his manacled arm and then up into the sheriff's face.

"No need to manhandle the lady," Jackson said pleasantly.

Looking dazed, Zack blustered, "Maybe the lady wants to be manhandled."

"She didn't seem willing from where I stood."

"No. I wasn't," Jessie said in a rush. "I've told Zack before...." She took a deep breath to calm her nerves before continuing. It was hard to be coherent when your wits were addled. And this unexpected savior had certainly scattered hers to the winds.

In the meantime, Zack's face darkened with frustration. "Why don't you tell the sheriff, Jessie, that this is a personal matter? We don't want to take up any more of his time."

For the first time, Jackson turned his full attention on her. "I don't believe we've been introduced, Ms. Reynolds. I'm Sheriff Wayne Jackson, at your service."

He tipped his hat in a deliberate way. "If I've interrupted something," he went on, "I'll be happy to leave."

"No," she said, instinctively edging closer to him. "I've told him before to keep his hands to himself."

She turned to Zack angrily. "Why can't you just take no for an answer?"

She turned back to the sheriff, knowing she was flushed, and that her voice revealed her fear. "Listen, Sheriff Jackson. Zack stepped way out of line, and he knows it. And I appreciate your efforts. But I'm not sure we need the law in on it."

"It's my duty to handle distress calls."

When Jackson smiled reassuringly, Jessie felt her heart turn over.

Old panic turned into a new alarm. This man was dangerous in a way Zack wasn't. He had broad shoulders, narrow hips and long muscular legs. And a smile that lit up a face chiseled from stone. He overloaded her sensory circuits.

"Now look here—" Zack tried to muscle between them.

With an easy motion, Jackson plucked him up and set him aside. "Now, Zack, ol' buddy, we need to reach an understanding. You've hired Ms. Reynolds to entertain the customers. Is that right, Ms. Reynolds?"

"Yes," Jessie said.

"But I don't think her contract gives you handling privileges. Does it, Ms. Reynolds?"

"No," she said vehemently.

"So if I were you—" Wayne moved in on Zack so the difference in their size was graphically illustrated "—I'd keep my hands to myself in the future. And," he continued, herding Zack toward the door, "I'd go back to the bar to show everyone the incident's over. I saw some mighty upset looks aimed your way."

Zack had no choice but to leave the office. He sent Jessie a surly look as he went.

Jackson turned back to her. There was a moment of silence while Jessie wondered what to say. She sensed a new tension in the room, very different from the resentment Zack had carried away with him. Jessie wasn't sure whether it came from herself or from Wayne.

"Thanks," she said and touched his arm lightly. "I said I could cool Zack down, and I can—usually. I feel stupid that you had to—"

"You shouldn't have to cool him down."

"—step in," she finished. "But I'm grateful for your help. I have to admit he caught me unexpectedly. At first, I didn't want to embarrass him."

"Is this something he tries on a regular basis?"

His brusque question wiped the smile off her face. She was suddenly aware of exactly where they were. Aware of the faint sounds of the crowd and band filtering into the office.

She was aware of the décolletage of her gown. Aware of the smell of smoke and beer permeating her elaborate hairdo. Aware that her stage makeup made her look like a high-class whore.

Awareness. That was the new tension she felt between them.

She tried to shrug it off. "You get used to aggressive males in my line of work." When he started to speak, she held out her hand. "Wait. Let me re-phrase my answer. In my line of work, I get used to fending off aggressive males. Diplomatically if pos-sible."

With her explanation, his face closed down. She couldn't begin to read what he was thinking.

When he spoke, his voice was just as impassive. "I assure you, Ms. Reynolds, I have no opinions about you or your line of work. I'm not much of a judge of country western music."

"Ouch!" she said. "I think I just got a negative review."

"Oh?"

This time her voice held a hint of provocation. "Most men have quite a few opinions at the end of one of my performances—about me and my mu-sic."

"Well, ma'am—" his voice was mild, his expres-sion bland "—I guess I'm not your average male customer. You know what they say about officers of the law. After a few years on the job, ice water flows through our veins."

"Do they really say that? How does your wife feel—?"

"I don't have one."

"Have you ever been married?" she asked, not-ing his clipped tone.

"I've been divorced for several years."

"Because of that ice water you mentioned?"

"Has anybody ever mentioned you're a nosy broad?"

Jessie broke into laughter at his unexpected retort. So—he didn't mind going on the offensive when necessary. This man was more complex than she would have guessed. And the encounter was unlike any she could remember.

"Why, Sheriff Jackson, I do believe I hit a sore spot." She poked his chest experimentally. "Although it's pretty hard to tell with that poker face you wear. Is it issued along with the uniform?"

"Objectivity's another thing we law officers aim for." His drawl was elaborate to the point of irony. "It doesn't pay to get involved with civilians."

So who asked him to get involved with anybody? Jessie thought. Backing away, she folded her arms and tilted her chin. "You don't have to worry," she said gently. "I haven't jumped a man in more than a week and a half."

Jackson turned red, surprising Jessie. A blush was the last thing she'd expected from him.

"I sure am glad you told me that," he drawled. "I was getting mighty nervous. After all, you practically come to my shoulder. And I can't outweigh you by more than a hundred or so pounds."

Since he chose to play it light, Jessie answered in a similar tone. "Well, you know what they say. The bigger they are, the harder they fall." She took several seconds to study him. "And when you fall they'd better yell 'Timber.'"

His lips twitched reluctantly. "Just make sure you don't get in the way."

She shook her head slowly and then finally admitted, "You know, Sheriff, I can't figure you out."

He smiled at her pleasantly. "Nobody asked you to, Ms. Reynolds."

"Ouch!" She cringed. "There you go again. Has something about me rubbed you the wrong way? Do you not like women? Or redheads?"

"I told you, it's not my job—" he began.

"Sheriff Jackson, it's too late to hide behind the badge."

"Then why don't you call me Wayne?" he countered. "Since we're not letting the badge come between us."

For the first time she was sure she heard irony in his voice.

"And I'm Jessie. That's what my friends call me." She held out her hand to him for shaking.

He stared at it broodingly.

"Aha," she said. "You've just proved my point. Sometimes, I have the feeling you enjoy the sparring. Then you freeze up like Han Solo in carbonite. Why don't you like me?"

"What's not to like? You're every man's fantasy."

"That bothers you, doesn't it?"

"Not in a crowd."

"What do you mean?"

He changed the subject. "Did you drive yourself here?"

"No. Zack brought me."

"When do you finish?" Wayne asked.

"I have a couple of sets. Another two hours."

"Wait for me. I'll be back to take you home."

"Do you really think that's necessary?"

"I'll ask you again—has Zack tried this before?"

"Yes." She blushed. "No," she corrected herself. "Not so aggressively."

"I see. Well—you may think you know how to fend off males. But I think you underestimate Zack's injured ego. When I called him off—"

"When you yanked him off is more like it."

"Exactly. No man enjoys looking small in front of a woman he has a yen for."

Before she could speculate on whether Wayne spoke from experience, he redirected her attention.

"In the meantime, lock your dressing room when you're in it. Don't let Zack corner you. And if he gives you any trouble, call this number right away. You got that?"

"Yes, sir!" She saluted. "I'm not as dense as Zack. I know orders when I hear them."

Wayne's eyes narrowed. "Zack may not be smart, but he knows what he wants. That's you, pretty lady, and I suspect he'll take you however he can get you. So instead of trying to be clever, exercise a little caution."

Jessie flushed at the rebuke, repressing the urge to stick out her tongue at him. "I'm sorry," she muttered, "for being lippy. Or should I say thank-you for the gracious compliment you just bestowed upon me?"

"Just keep out of trouble until I get back."

ZACK'S PLACE had the same desolate air at closing time as every dance hall Jessie had ever played. Without the constant clink of glasses and babbling voices and music filling the empty spaces, the remnants of cigarette smoke cast a silent pall over the cavernous room.

Only a few customers remained, their party spirits lagging. No one was aware that the star of the evening sat finishing a late supper in the shadows at one of the corner tables. In a simple cotton dress, her hair drawn back and covered, she didn't even look glamorous enough to be one of Zack's waitresses. That and the shadows suited her fine.

She'd already watched Al's Country Swing Band put away their instruments and depart. The bartender was washing the last shot glasses. And Tiny had assured her Zack had left to go home an hour ago.

Tiny still guarded the entrance, however, and as soon as Wayne appeared, Tiny corralled him into conversation, which gave Jessie a second chance to look the man over.

She'd seen him from a distance, of course, before tonight's encounter. He'd come into the Longhorn for coffee and a meal, and Dottie had raved about him on more than one occasion. Yet somehow, Jessie hadn't anticipated the impact the man made. It had been a long time since she'd been so...disturbed by a man.

He made Tiny look like the runt of a litter. A chubby runt at that. There probably wasn't much difference in their weight. Wayne's was just distributed a little more spectacularly. He didn't have an ounce of fat on his outsize frame.

There was no way any woman could make him look small, either physically or emotionally. Jessie had the feeling he guarded against the possibility. He'd politely closed the door on her several times during their chat.

Not that Jessie minded his hands-off attitude. It was a refreshing change from the Zacks of the world. Besides, she didn't need a distraction at this stage of her career. She'd already been down the dreary road of casual sex, out-of-town lovers and one-night stands. She'd learned long ago that the loneliest place in the world to be was in bed with a stranger. No, the last thing she wanted was a casual affair. Affairs, casual or otherwise, didn't fit in with her schedule.

But the sheriff did intrigue her. And he sent mixed signals, as if he were intrigued by her in a reluctant way.

After five minutes or so, Tiny pointed to the table where she was waiting, and Wayne started toward her. She decided the least she could do was to meet him halfway.

SHE'D CHANGED out of her costume, Wayne noted, as she approached him. She seemed shorter without her stiletto heels. Her makeup was gone, exposing a dusting of freckles, and if anything she was more beautiful than when he'd last seen her. He took a deep breath, trying to keep the thought of her from going to his head.

"Ready?" he asked.

"Anytime," she answered. "You know, I'm sure Tiny or Al could have given me a ride to the motel."

"It would have been out of Al's way, and Tiny isn't off yet."

"Oh? Did you ask him?"

Was that a hint of disappointment he heard in her voice? "You forget," he said, "I patrol Crystal Creek. I drive by Dottie's every thirty minutes. And I swing by Zack's the nights I'm on duty."

"I've never seen you here before."

"I don't usually come in."

"I remember now. You don't have much interest in country western music."

"I don't have much of an ear, remember?"

Giving him a skeptical look, she murmured, "I suspect you're being kind. Too kind. I can still ask Tiny—"

"I told you I'd drive you home," Wayne interrupted briskly. "You're my responsibility."

"Gee, I love the way you say that, Sheriff Jackson. You make romantic chills go up and down my spine."

Hoping he hadn't blushed, Wayne grunted a reply and ushered her out the door, waving to Tiny one last time.

Once they were in the parking lot and Wayne had more control, he again glanced down at her. "I'm a lawman, Jessie. I think in terms of responsibility."

"I know. It's just that you don't leave a girl many illusions."

"You're the one who deals in illusions."

"Only onstage. But see, offstage I'm just like everybody else."

He halted in his tracks and stared at her in the half darkness. "You couldn't be like anybody else if you tried."

While she stood looking startled by his comment, he went to the patrol car and opened the door for her.

After a moment she followed him. "I still can't tell," she muttered as she slid into the seat, "whether you're complimenting or criticizing me."

"I doubt that it matters." He closed the door on any retort she might have. Skirting the front end, he climbed into the cruiser and started the engine. "Did Zack behave himself?"

"He sulked for a while and then left," she said, apparently resigned to the change of subject.

"How are you getting to Zack's Place tomorrow evening?"

"I'm not. This was my last night."

"Good," Wayne said with heartfelt sincerity.

Jessie grinned. "Why, Sheriff? You anxious to get the wicked lady out of town? To stop her stirring up the menfolk?"

"You do that, all right."

"You said that before. You know, Sheriff, I'm really quite harmless. The sexy lady you met before is just part of a performance."

"The hell it is. You pour every ounce of yourself into your singing. You're probably more real performing than you are here with me."

She didn't speak for a moment, and he sensed she wasn't happy with his candor or his astuteness. Had he possibly hurt her?

"It's true," she finally said. "There is an intensity to my work. If I didn't care, the audience wouldn't."

"After seeing you, I'd say performing's your life."

"And composing." Her chin tilted upward. "I wouldn't have it any other way."

"In other words, nothing and nobody will stand between you and your career."

"You make me sound unscrupulous," she said. "I'd never shove someone aside to get where I wanted to go." She paused. "Sheriff—is it just me or do these chats of ours strike you as unusual? I mean, I don't ordinarily trade insults the very first date.''

Wayne cursed himself for the way he'd lost control of the situation. The problem was that when she sat this near him, his hormones took over and he went a little insane. Just as he'd been afraid would happen.

And he had hurt her. He couldn't deny it. He'd seen the shock in her eyes, even though she'd given as good as she'd got.

"Look," he said with a sigh. "I apologize if I—"

"Misjudged me?"

"If you're confused or hurt by anything I've said."

"Do you call that an apology?" she asked indignantly.

"Okay, okay. I'm sorry if I misjudged you. You're a very talented lady."

He shifted gears and pulled out of the parking lot, effectively cutting off conversation. Jessie stared out the windshield, trying to reclaim her thoughts.

CHAPTER TWO

THEY DROVE the next few minutes in silence. The car windows were open, and the warm summer night blew by Jessie's face. It was a welcome change from the stale, refrigerated air of the dance hall and seemed to clear her mind.

"Look," she said. "I'm sorry, too, if I've needled you. I really do appreciate your help this evening."

The last thing she expected to hear was a chuckle.

"Now what's the matter?" Her voice rose. "What have I said that's so funny?"

Wayne didn't answer until he'd stopped in front of the Longhorn Motel and Coffee Shop. He turned off the engine and looked at Jessie. "Nothing's the matter. I was laughing at myself and the situation. It's been an honor meeting you, Ms. Reynolds. I wish you the best in your career."

"You mean, here's my hat. What's my hurry?" Jessie scooted out of the passenger seat, then leaned back through the window. "It's been nice chatting with you, Wayne. Keep the peace and have a nice life."

THE TELEPHONE was ringing as she unlocked the door to the motel suite.

In her haste to answer it, she didn't seem to notice that Wayne had followed her in. He watched thoughtfully as she spoke into the receiver.

"Hello?...Nora?" Jessie's voice sharpened. "What's wrong?"

She listened a minute longer. "Shall I come down?...I know, but I'm not that tired. Are you sure? All right, you're probably right. But first thing in the morning I'll be there. Oh—okay. Call me if...when...I'll see you tomorrow here or in Austin. Tell Dottie I love her. And Nora—thanks for letting me know."

Jessie hung up the phone, turned and saw Wayne.

"Dottie collapsed at the café," she said. "She's had a heart attack. It happened several hours ago. She's in intensive care."

"At Crystal Creek Hospital?"

Jessie nodded. "As soon as it's safe, they'll take her into Austin to the cardiac care unit. I wanted to go sit with them, but Nora said I should wait and spell them later."

Jessie sank down into the chair by the phone. "I was at the café before I went to work. Dottie was laughing and talking. She seemed fine."

Wayne was silent. Then he moved to the telephone. After calling someone—his deputy, she supposed—he went into the kitchenette.

"You want some coffee?" he asked. "Do you have decaffeinated?" He opened the pantry and brought out a cardboard carton. "Or how about hot tea?"

She looked his way, barely comprehending what he was saying. "What?"

He held up the teapot he'd found on the hot plate.

"Oh. Yes. I drink herbal tea before I go to bed. But you don't have to fix it. I'm okay. The call from Nora was just so unexpected. It hit me kind of hard."

He grinned lopsidedly. "You might say it hit me hard, too. Maybe—" he located two mugs in the dish drainer by the sink "—I'm the one who needs a cup of something."

"Of course," Jessie said, noticing for the first time how bleak his expression was. "Please, help yourself. I'll have some tea."

He puttered around the cramped space, and she had the feeling he was trying to reclaim his composure.

"Dottie," he said at last, "was one of the first people to befriend me when I came to Crystal Creek. Once I passed muster with her, everyone else made me welcome. She also helped me understand small-town life."

"Had you never lived in a small town?"

"No."

When nothing else was forthcoming, Jessie broke the silence. "Dottie's always saying how lucky the town was to get you. Says as soon as she met you, she told Sheriff Nelson he'd found the right person to take over his job."

"Did she?" Wayne chuckled softly. "That's just like Dottie. Martin Avery may be the mayor, but Dottie's the one who looks after the town. I'll have to thank her the next time I see her."

They realized simultaneously the uncertainty of that event.

Jessie shook her head, still disbelieving. "I didn't have any idea she had a heart condition."

"Dottie might not have known it herself."

"If she did, she wouldn't have told anybody. She isn't much for complaining."

"But she's always ready to find out how the other person's doing. She knows whatever's going on."

"And she'll even gossip if she knows it's harmless." Jessie grinned at her memories. "I store up juicy industry tidbits to share with her whenever I come to visit. She wants to hear the songs I've written. Which towns I've played."

"She sounds like one of your fans."

"I'm one of hers, too. I've never met a more generous person. The way she welcomed Nora and Rory. The other people she's helped. She'd take in half the world if she had the rooms for it."

"Did Dottie take you in?" Wayne asked.

"In a way. She knows I'm on my own and miss my family."

"You live alone?"

"Yes." Jessie glanced his way, but his expression was impassive. "Anyway—I've filled Dottie's ear with my childhood and relatives."

"What about them?"

"The usual. I have a very average family."

"You don't know how rare an average family is."

Something in his voice cued her that his wasn't a casual remark.

"Well," she said, "mine's pretty rare then. Dad's a plumber in Monroe, Louisiana. Mom helps him with the accounting now that we kids are grown."

"Two parents, one marriage. That is unusual these days."

"They've been married thirty-five years." Jessie didn't try to keep the pride and affection out of her voice.

"How many kids?"

"Two brothers and me."

"Do you get to see them often?"

"Once or twice a year. Every spring if I can manage it. Monroe is beautiful in the springtime."

"You sound as if you miss it."

"I do. Although I was glad to escape."

"Escape?" He said the word as though he found it mildly distasteful.

"You know," she said, "to seek my fortune. Outside the church choirs, there isn't a big market for singers in Monroe. Anyway, whenever I get homesick I drive here from Austin and Dottie gives me a family fix."

"Don't you have to work in Nashville to become a country western star?"

"I may end up there, eventually. Right now Austin suits me fine. Some people call it the Live Music Capital of the World. Because of all the clubs that headline live entertainment. When I'm in town I work with some of the best." She frowned. "Of course, I'm on the road a lot."

His expression changed, but she couldn't read it.

"That's another reason," she explained, "Dottie means so much to me. When you're traveling week after week from one gig to another, long-term relationships are hard to come by."

"I went on the road when I played professional football. It's hell."

"You were in the NFL?" That would explain his sculptured physique and commanding presence.

"For three years," he answered, "until my knee went out."

"Couldn't they fix it?"

"They did. But by then I'd sat on the bench long enough to know I wanted out for good."

"Don't you miss the fame and fortune?"

"Never."

"So you know show business isn't as glamorous as people think."

"I was a cop in Las Vegas before I came here," he told her flatly. "I have no illusions about show business." He handed her a mug of steaming tea.

She murmured her thanks and sipped from it slowly, watching him cautiously put his lips to his cup. Did he have any idea how sensual his mouth was?

"So," she said, "you came to Texas looking for a quieter life."

"When you're the county's chief law officer, your life's never quiet. But I did come looking for real people and real values. And real day-to-day friendships."

"So you wouldn't have to snatch at them the way I do."

"I never want to snatch at anything or anyone again." His voice held bitterness. "I want people I can count on. People like Dottie."

But how much longer would Dottie be with them? Wayne must have had the same thought, because his mouth tightened.

"Even a community like Crystal Creek," Jessie said, "has its share of iniquity and sin."

"Are you comparing Crystal Creek to Las Vegas?" He laughed shortly.

"No. Of course not. I was just making a point." She sighed. "Oh, I don't know what I was doing. Keeping my mind off Dottie, I guess."

Wayne's expression softened. He hesitated for a moment. "I need to get going. Are you going to be all right alone?"

These days she spent half her time alone, but she didn't want to say it. She didn't want for him to think that she was bothered by the fact.

"Sure," she said instead. "I'm okay, now. It just took me a few minutes to adjust. I'll head for bed as soon as you walk out the door."

Wayne rinsed out his cup and donned his Stetson. "I plan to run by the hospital. If anything changes, I'll let you know."

"I'd appreciate that. And thanks again for everything, Wayne— Sheriff Jackson." She followed him to the door.

Before he went out into the night, he turned and smiled. "I thought you didn't intend to let the badge stand between us."

The badge was nothing, Jessie thought. This man's demons guarded him more vigilantly than any bronze star.

"Well, you know how it is." She made a pert face at him. "I don't want you to think I'm forward. I mean, you already have a bad impression of us show-biz types."

Shoving him gently out the door, she waved goodbye and bolted the latch, pleased she'd managed the last word.

ABOUT AN HOUR after Wayne left, Jessie realized sleep was out of reach, at least for the time being.

Perhaps she should brew another cup of chamomile tea. But she was too exhausted to crawl out of bed. Instead, she lay in the darkness, tired and wakeful.

Thoughts of Dottie crowded into her mind. Dottie's supportive attitude. Her plain speaking. What would Jessie do if she didn't have Dottie to talk to?

Jessie forced her thoughts in another direction. When she did, however, a menacing Zack appeared in her mind.

He'd manhandled her tonight. She'd felt the force of his insistence. She'd felt his refusal to acknowledge her protests. If they'd been alone, she wasn't sure how far he would have tried to go.

When she went back to Austin, she'd ask Todd to cancel future engagements at Zack's Place. Todd wouldn't like it. He hated to lose a performance fee. But he was, after all, her agent. She did have some say-so in her own career.

Having decided that, her mind began drifting. The darkness enfolded her like a soft woven shawl. Then the sheriff's face blotted out the random images. And the shawl was ripped away, leaving the unknown night.

Jessie felt her hands clench under the sheet. She pulled them out and shook them, trying to make them relax.

Where had her composure and objectivity vanished? The man wasn't even handsome. His features were too angular. Besides, handsome was a paltry term to describe the impression he left.

Her breath came out in jerks, and she forced herself to measure her air as though she were singing.

Sure he was bigger than life—but in a perfectly human way. Too human. Too compelling. He was just a county sheriff. She'd met more "important" people. But no one who radiated his strength and vitality. No one who seemed more comfortable with his vocation and terrain. No one whose rare smile shot through her like lightning.

Jessie realized her pulse was throbbing. She could feel it in her throat and against the walls of her chest. Her reaction to the man bewildered her. And her behavior had reflected her confusion. One minute she'd been a flirt, the next minute she'd acted like a sulky child.

She'd teased him—trying to trigger a response. But after she'd provoked it, she'd not known what to do next.

She suspected Wayne considered her an annoying distraction. Staring into the gloom at the featureless ceiling, she tried to remember if she'd ever before been considered an annoyance.

No. It was a unique experience. One she didn't care to repeat.

Not that Wayne wasn't attracted to her. After all, eliciting desire was part of her stock-in-trade. But unlike other men, Wayne considered his hankering a character defect. At least, that was how she read his ambivalence.

It was just as well their paths would seldom cross in the future. Really, all they had in common was Dottie.

Dottie.

Sighing, Jessie threw off the covers and groped for her slippers. Another cup of tea was definitely called for.

When the teakettle whistled, Jessie rinsed her cup and poured the hot water over a fresh tea bag. Then she carried her cup to the coffee table in front of the couch. She opened the guitar case that lay on the table. Lifting out her acoustic, she settled its leather strap around her neck. When she was in this kind of mood, composing was the only solution.

Besides, she could hear in her mind the beginnings of a song. A song about loneliness. Or was it about losing someone? Someone unexpected.

Sitting Indian fashion on the couch, she riffled the pick over the strings, tuning and adjusting them, pausing to take a sip of her tea.

She thought she had the first line.

"I didn't understand that I could lose you...."

Or should it be... "I'd planned my tomorrows with you in mind...?"

Within moments she was lost in her work.

WAYNE COULD HEAR HER through the door. But she must not have heard his knock above the chords she was playing. He knocked harder.

The chords stopped. After a second, he heard a scuffling noise and sensed her peering out her peephole. The door opened quickly to reveal her ashen face.

She knew the reason he was here. He could see her dread and apprehension.

But he had to say it. "Dottie is dead."

Jessie stepped back blindly, shaking her head in denial and clutching her guitar as if she were trying to shield herself with it.

When she backed into the coffee table, he caught her arm to steady her. It seemed like the safest thing was to lift the instrument from around her neck.

"When?" she asked, a tremor in her voice.

"Not long after I got there," he answered.

"Couldn't they take her to Austin?"

"Her condition never stabilized enough to make the trip."

"I know, but—"

"Her heart stopped beating again, Jessie," he said gently.

"Couldn't they—"

"This time, nothing they tried could save her."

"I should have gone to the hospital."

"It wouldn't have changed things."

Jessie brought a trembling hand to her face. "But I never got the chance to say goodbye. Nora. Poor Nora. How is she taking it?"

Wayne remembered the anguish he'd left at the hospital. "About as well as can be expected." He changed his answer. "Pretty hard. She and Dottie were very close."

"And Rory?"

"He doesn't know yet."

"To lose his grandmother—so soon after his father." Jessie covered the sob that came from her throat.

"I knew—after you left," she said, her voice barely above a whisper. "Somewhere deep inside I knew she wouldn't make it. These past few months must have been too much for her. That's—that's why—" she gestured futilely at the guitar. "I tried working. The music usually helps."

Only a lamp illuminated their figures. But Wayne could see her body begin to tremble.

Without another thought he put his arms around her, sheltering her close against his chest.

"I—I'm sorry," she chattered and clutched at his shirt. "I can't understand it. I d-don't usually go to pieces."

"It's been a long night."

She stared up at him, moisture filling her eyes. "It's—it's been a long night for you, too. I know what Dottie m-meant to you. You've known her a lot longer than I have."

"Hey," he said softly, cradling her head with his fingers, breathing in the scent of her sweet-smelling hair. "We're not having a contest to see who hurts the most. And you don't have to apologize for crying."

"Even if it's all over your uniform?"

"The uniform washes. It's seen tears before."

"I guess it has." She lifted her face again to study him. "You must have to deal with death often in your line of work."

He tensed. "Too often. And it never gets easier."

She laid her cheek against him as if she needed to hear his beating heart. "Oh, Wayne," she said with a sigh. "How could this have happened? It affects so many people."

His hold tightened. "Who ever knows the reasons? Maybe—maybe her heart had already been broken."

"Because of her son?"

"Yes."

"She never said anything negative about Gordon. Yet she must have felt horrible about what he'd done."

"Maybe she'd held her love inside even after Gordon had shattered it." Wayne knew how it felt when love shattered. He knew the jagged pain.

"Maybe," he said, "she just wore out with the effort."

"Are you saying this was inevitable?"

"No. Only that events aren't as chaotic as they seem."

"Do you think our lives are preordained? That everything that happens to us was meant to be? Do you think we have a choice?'' Her voice was growing fuzzy.

He tried to gather himself to loosen his hold. ''Now you've turned philosophical. I don't have answers there, either.''

''But haven't you ever wondered? No. Don't let go...you feel so nice.'' She wrapped her arms around him. ''So solid...so gentle. Has anyone ever told you you do good work? People must lean on you a lot. No wonder you make a good sheriff. I bet people come to you all the time....'' Her breath caught on a sob. ''I'm going to miss Dottie.''

He had no choice but to gather Jessie closer, one hand cradling her head, the other soothing the slope of her spine. His own body was torn between grief, pleasure and panic. Draped around him, she felt as lush as he'd imagined when he listened to her sing.

Yet the images he remembered were from another life. The life that had ended with Dottie's death.

Dottie was irreplaceable. But he'd had practice in losing irreplaceable things.

''Wayne...?''

''Hmmm?''

''I feel light-headed.''

''It's reaction.''

''Like I'm going to faint.''

''I've got you. Don't worry.''

When her arms started to slide from around him, he picked her up and went to lay her in bed. Maybe she'd sleep with the tension drained away.

He pulled the sheet from underneath her and covered her, shielding her body from his gaze. Now that he wasn't holding her, he shuddered.

He wasn't in much better shape than she was. His defenses were tattered. At the hospital Nora and the others had needed his strength and solace. But being comforting and strong exacted its own toll.

Looking down on the woman he meant to keep at a distance, Wayne would have liked nothing better than to strip off his clothes and climb in beside her, breathing in the scent of her, dispensing with her nightgown, pulling her to him, drawing on her warmth and tenderness to help him through the night.

This time his shudder seemed to possess him completely.

"Wayne?"

"I thought you were asleep."

"I was, kind of. But I knew you were there."

Unable to resist, he smoothed a strand of hair from her forehead.

"For such a large man," she murmured, "you have the gentlest touch."

"When you're as big as I am, you have to be gentle."

"Not with Zack, you weren't."

"I don't mind throwing my weight around when necessary. Size has its value."

"Wayne..." Her eyelids were drooping. "Thank you for coming to tell me about Dottie. I seem to be saying thank-you a lot."

"Don't talk. Go to sleep," he directed her softly.

But instead of following directions, she reached out her hand. "Are you okay?" she asked. "Do you have someone to talk to?"

Her questions hit him unexpectedly.

"I'm okay," he muttered.

Once she was reassured, her eyelids closed and she began to breathe rhythmically.

He waited another minute or two, wanting to be certain she was sleeping. Once assured of that, he went hurriedly into the night.

When he reached the cruiser, he jerked open the door, climbed in and slammed it behind him.

"Hell!" He spit out the lamentation.

There wasn't any point in having someone to talk to. Because "hell" was all he could think of to say.

CHAPTER THREE

THE DAY of Dottie's funeral dawned in typical August fashion. By the 11 o'clock service at the First Baptist Church, the temperature had already topped ninety degrees. Since rainfall had been scarce the past month, the creek bed winding through town had dried up, and a fine chalky dust had settled over the wilted foliage. Only the crape myrtle bushes on the church lawn had the energy to bloom. They were a touch of bright color contrasting with the muted shades of grief.

Mercifully, the sanctuary had been air-conditioned, but now at the cemetery, the sun beat down on the congregation. Even protected by the canvas canopy, the minister and Dottie's relatives were scorched by the fitful wind.

Jessie stood outside the canopy in a cluster of townspeople, listening to Reverend Blake's fluid voice mingling with the sounds of soft crying. Within minutes, her dark dress was stuck to her damp skin. Sweat trickled down her cheeks, blending with the teardrops. Unruly strands of hair clung to the nape of her neck.

Yet she scarcely noticed the discomfort. She concentrated on Reverend Blake's words.

"...We commend to Almighty God our sister, Doris Jones; and we commit her body to the ground; earth to earth, ashes to ashes, dust to dust. The Lord bless her and keep her, the Lord make his face to shine upon her and be gracious unto her, the Lord lift up his countenance upon her and give her peace. Amen."

Dottie had come to rest beside Gordon, her son.

The live oaks sheltering the graves on either side quaked in a strong gust of wind, and a sudden chill of despair shuddered through Jessie.

Death was so final. So absolute. So immutable. She, who had always believed in being the master of her fate, felt an unfamiliar helplessness. And a new sense that events beyond her control could rupture her life.

Yet she felt more than despair and loss. She was moved by the tributes Dottie's memory had evoked. Martin Avery's eulogy, the abundance of flowers, the packed sanctuary, the crowd outside the church, listening to the service on the loudspeaker system.

As everyone had gathered at the grave site, Jessie hadn't recognized many of the mourners. But she knew enough to spot the McKinneys and the Townsends. And she'd heard enough about Hank Travis, the family patriarch, to know how honored Dottie would have been that he'd attended her last rites.

In deference to his age, he'd been given a seat with the family. She could see him now from where she stood. His body was worn with age, yet his back was ramrod straight, his head unmoving. His thoughts were a secret behind his wizened face.

Jessie also recognized several of the Longhorn's habitués. Friends Dottie had introduced to her. Vernon Trent, Cody Hendricks, Manny Hernandez, Bubba Gibson.

Jessie herself had been recognized as well. Before the service, Eva Blake, the preacher's wife, had welcomed her. And as people mingled with one another, speaking quietly, sharing reminiscences, several came by to tell Jessie how often Dottie had spoken of her.

"In fact," Beverly Townsend told Jessie, "Dottie said you were the reason people were listening to the jukebox."

Just then Mary Gibson came up to introduce herself as one of Dottie's close friends. "I bet you didn't know Dottie had begun a scrapbook for you."

Jessie shook her head. "I had no idea."

"She was going to give it to you some day as a present. So that you could retrace your steps along the road to fame."

When Mary said that, Jessie didn't have words to express her gratitude. The two women hugged each other instead.

The small band of relatives had formed a line in front of the casket while friends and neighbors passed by to offer condolences. As Martin Avery came by he confided to Marge, Dottie's sister from Dallas, "You know, Dottie said, when I revised her will, that when the Lord called her, she hoped it would be in August, so she wouldn't mind hightailing it up to heaven."

That drew a smile from Marge, Jessie and the others. Jessie realized suddenly that Dottie would have wanted joking at her funeral. She'd always said life was leavened with a laugh.

"She'd lived in Texas all her life," Marge said, "but she never got used to the summers. She always said—" Marge's voice broke for a moment "—she always said she was going to sell the Longhorn and live in the mountains. But we all knew better."

Doc Purdy took Marge's hand. "I think Dottie was exactly where she wanted to be."

"I know." Marge hugged the doctor. "And thank you for doing all you could. I know how hard the night of her death was on you."

"That's what I get for practicing in Crystal Creek. When I lose a patient, I also lose a friend."

Jessie followed the doctor, shaking hands with Marge and her husband, approaching Nora and Ken, who stood with Rory between them. Rory clutched Ken's pant leg, leaning into the security of his body. Jessie had to blink back moisture at the scene.

"Nora—" Jessie had prepared a small speech, saying how much Dottie had meant to her. But somehow she couldn't get the words past her constricted throat.

Nora seemed to understand. She reached out her arms to Jessie, and the two embraced.

Eventually, the relatives were ushered to the waiting limousines, and the crowd dispersed. As the cemetery settled to a somber silence, Jessie was left once more feeling like an outsider.

Everyone had been thoughtful, including her in the memories. But Dottie belonged to Crystal Creek. Jessie could only claim a small piece of her. Yet the void Dottie's death had left in Jessie's life seemed enormous.

While the cemetery employees waited to lower the coffin into the grave, Jessie smoothed her fingers one last time over the flower-laden casket. When she turned to go, she bumped into Wayne.

She'd noticed him earlier. It was impossible not to. In a suit and tie, he looked appropriately solemn and surprisingly elegant.

"Are you going by Dottie's house?" he asked, steadying her. "That's where people are gathering for lunch."

"I don't know. If I could help in the kitchen, I would. But I'm sure the family has more volunteers than it knows what to do with. Nora said enough food has arrived to feed an army for a week."

He looked around. "Where's your car?"

"At the church. I drove over here with Billie Jo and Mary Alice." Jessie glanced around. "Oh, no—they seem to have left without me."

"I'll take you," he said.

Something in his voice made her say, "You don't need to." She glanced around in hopes of finding other transportation.

"What am I supposed to do?" he asked dryly. "Leave you by yourself looking lonely and sad?"

She smiled at him weakly. "I wasn't so much lonely—"

"As feeling left out?"

"How did you know?"

"I feel the same way." As he spoke, he directed Jessie to a battered pickup truck. "Dottie is part of Crystal Creek history. I'm only a footnote."

Jessie stopped to study him musingly. "You know, for a sheriff you're surprisingly eloquent."

"Surprisingly?"

"Well, you know—one doesn't usually think of a cop..."

His lips twitched briefly. "It must be all those reports I have to write."

Before he slid into the truck, he signaled to his deputy, who'd led the cortege. Returning the wave, the officer left in the black-and-white.

Climbing in the passenger side, Jessie almost choked on the stale hot air.

Before she shut the door, Wayne had already turned a knob and they were hit with a blast of air-conditioning.

"Ah, heaven," she crooned, lifting her mass of hair from her shoulders. After a moment, she said, "You always picture funerals taking place in the rain. But heat's just as fitting. It's more like the grief you feel inside."

"There's more than one kind of grief."

The way he said the words caused her to look at him in question.

"Bitter grief can be hot and angry. Resignation is usually as cold as the grave. If you're lucky you can let go of both and find resolution."

"You sound like you know what you're talking about."

"I do."

After a moment of silence, she asked, "Did you learn all this from your divorce?"

"Partly. Divorce is a kind of death, take it from me." His tone was hard-edged.

"I guess it is." She swallowed hard. "Mine was a nosy question. I think you bring the nosiness out in me."

"Wait a minute. I refuse to take the rap for your curiosity."

His light tone gave her the courage to say, "But you keep making cryptic statements. How can I help but be curious? Besides," she went on, "Dottie's the first person I've lost this way. None of my family's ever died—except for my great-grandma.''

''You're fortunate.''

''I know,'' she said. ''But I'm also unprepared.''

''What do you want? Lessons in grieving?''

''No. No, of course not. I didn't mean it that way. It's just—you don't sound as if you've had it... easy.''

''No one does—over the long haul.''

''What about the short haul?''

His look met hers for an instant before he returned his attention to the road. ''Just what do you want to know, Jessie?''

''The same things you asked me the other night. Is—is most of your family still living?''

''I have no family.''

''Oh. I see. I'm sorry.''

He slowed the truck to make the turn into the church parking lot. He pulled to a halt beside the Dodge Colt she'd pointed out to him.

''No need to be sorry,'' he said. ''And you're right, I did ask about your family. My father left when I was a kid. I don't know what became of him. My mother died later.''

''How much later?''

''When I was nine.'' His voice was matter-of-fact as though he were speaking of another person.

''Didn't you have anyone else? Grandparents? Aunts and uncles?''

''None I ever knew of.''

"You mean at nine years old you were an orphan?"

"I guess you could look at it that way. Although I'd learned to take care of myself long before then."

"But what happened to you? I mean, you couldn't live alone."

"I went through a series of foster homes. When my last foster father died, they put me in a group home."

"That must have been hard for you. How did you make it?"

He shrugged. "I had help along the way. And some people are just survivors."

He stretched his arm along the seat back, and his gaze met hers directly. His expression seemed to hold a subtle challenge, as if he understood the effect his story had had on her.

"Anything else you need to know?" he asked.

"No." She already knew too much for her peace of mind.

Opening the door, she prepared to leave. Suddenly it hit her how much she'd miss his company, however contrary it had been.

"I'm going to miss Dottie very much." Jessie paused. "Well—I guess I'll take off." She swung her feet out onto the asphalt.

"Are you driving into Austin today?"

She nodded. "I have to. I start a gig at Kickers tonight."

"Are you going by Dottie's first?" he asked for the second time.

Her look wandered over the church, the crape myrtle, the empty parking lot, the education building. "I don't guess I will."

"You want to stop by my office for a cup of coffee?"

Twisting around to face him, she asked, "Is it so obvious that I'm scared to be alone?"

"We all are," he assured her. "Why do you think I extended the invitation? Why do you think people come together after a funeral? All of us can use the emotional support. Come with me to Dottie's. I'll drop you off at your car later."

She took a deep breath. "I would like some coffee."

"And lunch. It's after one o'clock."

"So it is." Maybe it was hunger pangs knotting her stomach. "Okay. We'll go together." She swung her feet back into the cab.

Starting the truck, he nodded in satisfaction.

THREE HOURS LATER they left the house where Dottie had lived. Jessie was tired but less melancholy. It had been good for her to participate in this last ritual of grief.

"Thank you for making me go," she said to Wayne as he drove back to the church.

"I didn't make you."

"Thank you for encouraging me."

"You're welcome."

"No wonder you love Crystal Creek."

His glance was questioning. "Where did that come from?"

"Oh, I don't know. It's just that these people have such an acceptance and understanding of life and death. I'm writing a song about it, but I'm not sure yet what I'm trying to say."

"Do you compose all the songs you sing?"

"Most of them. I also sell my songs to other performers. Clyde Miller's made one the lead cut on his album. Oh, I forgot, you don't know much about country performers."

"That's right."

"I'll have to educate you. I mean, after all—" she sent him a grateful smile "—it's the least I can do after the way you've befriended me."

He didn't respond.

"Of course," she went on, "I won't be in town as often without Dottie to visit. And I've asked Todd, my agent, to negotiate me out of my contract with Zack."

"Good."

"But I'm driving up in a couple of weeks to visit Nora. She has some of Dottie's things to give me." Blinking back tears, Jessie added, "Why don't I call you, and we'll do lunch?"

He pulled up beside her car and killed the engine to the truck. "I don't think so," he said, staring out the front window.

"Don't play hard to get, Sheriff. I'll buy. Even I can swing Sonny's Barbecue Buffet."

"No, thank you." His tone was flat.

"Oh, come on. Don't be so ornery."

He turned to face her and said abruptly, "You don't get it, do you? You and I can never be friends."

"Don't you think that's a bit strong, Sheriff Jackson?" she said, trying not to show how his words hurt her. "I know our early going's been a little rocky. But I like to think we've reached an understanding."

"We haven't reached anything, dammit." He hit the steering wheel with his fist.

"Why are you so angry? All I'm saying is, we should be friends."

"The hell you are."

"I don't know what you mean."

"Friendship," he said. "That's all you want from me?"

"Yes."

"Then why do you keep asking personal questions?"

"Well, I—"

"Why the flirting and teasing?"

"Now wait a minute—"

"Why can't you keep your eyes off me?"

Drawing up to her full height, she hissed, "You egotistical bastard."

"Maybe I am." His expression was hard. "But I know when a woman wants me."

"And I damn sure know when a man wants me."

"My point exactly."

"Oh, I see," Jessie said, after a moment. Her voice grew reasonable. "Then we don't have a problem. I have men friends who had certain ideas when they first met me. The more you get to know me, the less sexy I'll seem. The real me wears a potato sack to bed."

He laughed. It was a raw, husky, jagged sound that cut through her rationalizations.

"Do you really think it's as easy as that?" he asked. "Do you think it's as simple as a hard-on I get when you wiggle your behind? Or when your breasts jiggle in a slip of a gown? You think you don't look sexy to me in that excuse for a nightie I saw you in the other night? Well, think again."

He took hold of her arms and pulled her toward him. "You don't have any idea, lady, how much I want you."

She could see the hunger in his eyes and it made her light-headed.

"But I'm not going to take you." He pushed her away.

"Why?" Jessie's thoughts were confused, her emotions tangled. "Do I remind you of your ex-wife?"

His look flickered over her, contained once more. "No. She's prettier than you, for one thing. More delicate. She's a platinum blonde."

"I see."

"Don't be discouraged," he said dryly, "you got all the talent. Michelle couldn't kick her way into a Las Vegas chorus line."

"Does she want a career in show business?" Jessie asked.

"She'd gamble her soul for one. As it is, she's had to settle for being a blackjack dealer."

"And you blame her career dreams for your marital breakup?"

"No. No, I don't." For the first time, he sounded resigned. "We should never have married, I see that now. Michelle thought she'd hitched her star to my football career. I thought I was marrying a woman who wanted to stay home and make babies. I don't blame Michelle for our split-up, but I don't intend to ever repeat the mistake."

"With someone like me, you mean."

"Yes."

"You are egotistical. What makes you think I want to crawl into your bed? I had my fill of one-night stands a long time ago, buster. The last thing I need is a romp in the hay."

When he started to speak, she raised her voice. "You're right. I have God-given talent. And I plan to go as far as I can with it. I don't have any time to waste on a hick sheriff who's in the market for a maid and a baby factory. So if you thought—"

"It wasn't a matter of thinking."

"If you hoped—"

"You mean, if I feared—"

"Fine," she snapped. "Whatever you say."

Yet even as she spoke the words, desolation swept over her, sapping away the anger. She gazed out the windshield, with a new vulnerability. He had been her friend, in spite of his reluctance. She hadn't wanted to lose him. She hadn't known parting like this would hurt so much.

Groaning, he took hold of her shoulders. "Jessie, believe me. I know what's best."

"You're the sheriff. I guess you set the rules."

"Dammit. You don't know what you're doing. You don't understand."

She stared at him, wide-eyed, not sure what he wanted from her at this moment.

With a sigh, he drew her into his arms.

She shook with the contact. She could feel his body shaking. His hands swept over her back and into her hair.

Her head fell back, and the first place his lips touched her was along the slope of her throat. Everywhere their skin met, she wanted more.

She mewed in response, her body quickening. He pulled her closer still until she lay against him, his chest hard and solid beneath her breasts.

His desire burned her along the length of her thigh. Her nipples tightened with the tension inside her.

"You think we could work this out with a romp in the hay?" he rasped. "You think that would get you out of my system? Hell—I have to get you out of my life.''

Even as he spoke his intentions, his lips slid along her cheek, his breath whispering a promise. His tongue dipped inside as soon as his mouth covered hers.

Whimpering, she clasped her arms around his neck to urge him deeper. He moaned and her fingers dug into his hair.

She was adrift in a sea of sensual awareness. He was her only anchor. He was the only thing she wanted. He set her on fire with need.

"Damn." His breath labored, he pushed her away from him. "Damn." He drew back as far as he could. "Damn." He squirmed, pulling at his suit pants. "Damn." He leaned his head back and closed his eyes.

"I see what you mean," she whispered. "You want me out of your life."

"Yes."

"So you won't be tempted."

"So neither of us does something we'll regret."

"I liked you, you know. You made me feel safe."

Digging his hands through his hair, he snorted his amusement. "Honey, I'm probably the most dangerous man you'll ever know."

"But that's just it. I won't ever know you."

"Well," he said ironically, "that's the breaks of the game."

She stared at him silently. Even now he fascinated her. Especially now.

He'd made this decision unilaterally. She'd had no say in it. Just like Dottie's death, this ending was out of Jessie's hands.

For a moment, rebellion simmered inside her. There were ways—a woman's wiles. This parting didn't have to be final. For just an instant, she imagined a seduction, and her heartbeat quickened.

Reality slowed it down. He was right. Better to end it now.

"So this is goodbye," she said with determined cheerfulness. Climbing out of the truck, she hung on to her aplomb. She sure as hell wasn't going to let him see her vulnerable. That wasn't the memory she wanted him to carry.

Leaning back into the cab, she batted her lashes elaborately. "You know—I could have taught you a lot—about country western music."

He met her gaze head on. "And I could have taught you a lot—about desire."

In a flash, her aplomb was gone, swamped by a wave of resentment. "You bastard! You come on to me with friendship, then decide I'm too much woman for you. And you won't even let me have the last word."

She stomped to her car, his silence dogging her.

When tears streaked her face on the road back to Austin, she wasn't sure whether she was crying for Dottie or for the man she'd left behind.

CHAPTER FOUR

"SHERIFF—" Martin Avery hailed Wayne on the steps of the courthouse. "Got a minute? I was just coming to talk to you about Kenneth Thompson."

Wayne halted his progress to his waiting patrol car. "Sure. What do you need?"

"You know what I need," Martin said as soon as he caught up with Wayne.

"For me to persuade Cal Dawkins to drop charges against Kenneth."

"Dammit, Wayne. Cal wants Kenneth to face a count of felony car theft. The kid's only fourteen."

"Kenneth did take a joyride in Cal's brand-new Buick," Wayne pointed out.

"I know." Martin looked a little discouraged. "All the Thompsons tend to be a little wild."

"If Cal drops the charges, can you assure him Kenneth won't repeat the offense?"

"No," Martin confessed. "You know there's been bad blood between the Dawkinses and Thompsons ever since Kenneth's grandmother ran off with his grandfather while she was engaged to Cal's dad."

"Eugene Nelson told me about the squabble when I first got here," Wayne said. "And remember I broke up a fight between a Thompson and a Dawkins just last year. I think Crystal Creek and I have had about enough.''

"What are you saying?''

"If we're not careful Kenneth's going to end up in a whole lot of trouble. I don't like to lose a kid that way, especially not because of some Hatfield and McCoy–type feud. You and I are going to organize a peace conference, Martin.''

"Holy cow,'' Martin said. "Do you know what you're saying?''

Wayne grinned. "Yes, I do.''

"Eugene tried that once before.''

"We're going to try it again. I think now that you're mayor, you carry extra clout.''

"You mean Cal might be more likely to bow to public opinion?''

"Exactly.''

"What about the Thompsons?''

"I don't believe they want a boy of theirs to end up in Huntsville.''

"You're right.'' Martin sighed. "But I'm sure not looking forward to this. Old grudges die hard. The peace conference might not work, you know.''

"It won't work if we don't try.''

"I'm glad to see my client means that much to you, Sheriff.''

"Every kid means that much to me, Martin.''

The two men shook hands and made plans for a strategy session. Then Avery continued up the steps and Wayne made for his vehicle ready to begin his afternoon circuit. The route was varied to avoid predictability. But these afternoon runs were as dependable as the sun.

For the past five years, Wayne had worked to gain Claro County's confidence and respect. He'd learned as much as he could about the people who lived here and tackled other thorny problems like the Thompson/Dawkins feud. Once he assumed command, he'd made a well-run sheriff's department better. Now it ranked among the state's best.

When he was elected after Eugene's resignation, Wayne had known he was accepted for himself and not just as Eugene's protégé. He considered the trust he'd earned sacred. He had an obligation to Kenneth, to the Thompsons, to the Dawkinses and to all the other citizens he served. Crystal Creek was the first place that had ever made him feel as if he belonged.

Keeping the car windows open was standard procedure even in summer, and Wayne pulled up to the Dairy Bell drive-in window for a glass of iced tea. Sandy, a junior at Crystal Creek High, was eager to serve him. She had a crush on him, but there was nothing he could do about that.

Sandy's mother, Denise Cramer, was a different story. Widowed, a pretty woman in her thirties, she'd let him know on more than one occasion that she was interested and available.

He admired her for staying in Crystal Creek to raise her two children. He knew her job at Cal Dawkins's insurance company was just that, a job. He suspected she'd like nothing better than to marry again, live on a sheriff's salary and produce more children as he provided them. The lady was exactly what he was looking for. So why hadn't he asked her out?

All you want's a maid and a baby factory....

Wayne muttered under his breath and Sandy's eyes widened. Smiling a weak goodbye, he pulled out from the drive-in, cursing his errant thoughts.

It had been a week since Dottie's funeral. A week since he'd forced himself to do what he had to do. It had also been a week since he'd gotten a good night's sleep.

He couldn't remember the last time he'd lost sleep over anyone. Until this past week and a half, his life in Crystal Creek had been organized and serene.

Well, any minute, things would be getting back to normal. He fully expected to regain his equilibrium.

Only he wished he hadn't kissed her. Now he had a taste of what he'd denied himself. Hers was a taste that lingered on the senses. He could still feel her softness along the palms of his hands. He could recall her response in his aching groin.

Digging his hand through his hair in frustration, he turned onto the highway. *Better start thinking with your brain instead of your crotch for a change....*

Wayne took a route south out of town. He made his usual swing by Zack's Place. Only a few cars dotted the parking lot. The afternoon clientele included the serious drinkers, because whatever live entertainment Zack provided didn't come on until eight.

Who the hell was that?

He slowed to take a look at the unfamiliar vehicle parked near Zack's entrance. A Jaguar XJII. Which of Zack's customers could afford such a toy? According to the dealer's plate it had been purchased in Dallas. Someone from Dallas in a Jaguar just passing through?

Intrigued, he turned around and drove back by the nightclub just as two men walked out into the bright sunlight. Wayne was sure he was a half mile up the road by the time their eyes had adjusted to the glare. But he'd recognized them in an instant, and his mind had started racing.

What were a big-time Vegas gambler and his flunky doing at Zack's? That was a question Wayne meant to answer.

He drove on another five minutes expecting the Jag to overtake him, but apparently they'd headed toward San Antonio.

Making another U-turn, Wayne returned to Zack's. Tiny's Pontiac was parked around the side, which meant Tiny was on duty.

Wayne found the bouncer on the stool by the door.

"Why, Sheriff, good to see you," Tiny said. "Is this business or pleasure?"

"Oh, a little of both. Just stopped by to see if you'd had any trouble lately. Besides, it's hot enough outside to fry an egg over easy."

"Well, come on in and grab some cool."

"Having a slow afternoon?" Wayne asked, folding his arms and leaning against a table.

"Slow and peaceful. They way I like it."

"That's good to hear." Wayne paused before saying casually, "Hey—I saw a Jag in the parking lot a minute ago. Must have set somebody back close to a hundred grand."

"Yeah?" For the first time, Tiny's expression was leery.

"I guess it belonged to out-of-towners. Nobody in Crystal Creek has a set of wheels like that. Anybody we know?"

"Not really," Tiny mumbled.

"What did they order? Champagne and caviar?"

"They weren't interested in ordering. They went straight to Zack's office."

"Friends of his?"

"With friends like that he don't need enemies."

"Oh?" Wayne let his tone sharpen as he asked yet another question. "What do they want?"

"I'm not sure." Tiny glanced around. "Listen, Sheriff, I don't want to cause trouble. A guy like me sees a lot of things he don't mention to anyone. It comes with the territory."

Wayne nodded judiciously.

"But I have the feeling Zack's in over his head. I kind of like the guy, even if he is a sleaze ball. He's been good to me, hiring me like he did."

"I understand."

"So...well...if you'd keep your eyes open. I'm not sure how to say this, but he may need help."

"He may not be able to use my help." Wayne chose his words carefully. "He might not be in a position to call on the law."

"Yeah," Tiny said. "You may be right. But I hate to see them put the squeeze on him."

"Listen," Wayne said. "I realize the position you're in."

"I need this job, Sheriff. I got a wife and three kids to support."

"I hear you. And I won't ask you to jeopardize your paycheck. But if you'd keep your eyes open, too, just in case..." Wayne trailed his words off, waiting to see if Tiny picked up on them.

"You mean in case I see anything screwy?"

"If you do, I'd appreciate your letting me know."

"Okay," Tiny said with a sigh of resignation.

Wayne gave him an approving nod. "And if something's going down, don't get mixed up in it. Don't get caught in the same vise as Zack, if you know what I mean."

"I know what you mean." Tiny's look met Wayne's.

Wayne laid a hand on Tiny's shoulder. "I knew you would."

ON THE WAY back to the office, Wayne added up what he knew.

First of all, Zack was a football fanatic obsessed by both the NFL and the college game. Every wall in Zack's Place was covered with football paraphernalia and autographed pictures of Texas celebrities from Bobby Layne to Earl Campbell to the world-champion Dallas Cowboys.

Not only that, he kept up with teams and their personnel. He was one of the few people in Crystal Creek who knew Wayne was a has-been tight end. Wayne's career had been too short to be memorable. But a gambler used to studying the rosters would have known his position.

Wayne had heard when he'd first arrived in Crystal Creek that Zack gambled. He'd assumed, as Eugene had, that the gambling was minor league. But if Zack's visitors were any indication, he could be getting in over his head as Tiny had said.

Wayne pulled into his parking slot and went into the wing of the courthouse occupied by the sheriff's offices. When he walked in, he found Roy and the dispatcher, Alberta, sorting through the Wanted posters.

He'd inherited them both from Eugene. Alberta was efficient, although occasionally cantankerous and not always as discreet as she should be. Roy was a good, steady, plodding deputy, who'd never had any aspiration to become sheriff. He was more than happy to take orders from Wayne.

"Anything interesting out there today?" Roy asked.

"As a matter of fact..."

Wayne's conditional answer caught their attention.

Wayne, however, took the time to hang his hat on the coatrack and sink down in a comfortable chair.

"Well?" Roy prodded him.

"First tell me what you know about Zack's gambling."

Roy looked surprised and then he squirmed uncomfortably. "Oh—well—the same as everyone else. He's always good for a little action. Not that I go in for any."

"Relax, I'm not trying to trip you up. I just wondered if you'd heard anything about the action lately. Has he set up an operation? Do I have a gambling ring to flush out?"

"Not that I know of. He's always been small potatoes. Sheriff Nelson decided that years ago. If I heard anything different I would have come to you, Wayne."

Noting Roy's anxious face, Wayne said, "I know you would have."

"Then why are you asking these questions?"

"I'll tell you as soon as I get more information." Wayne turned to Alberta. "Call Gilbert and Bobby and ask them to come in. We need a conference. But first, let me check something out.''

He went into his private office and dialed long distance to the Las Vegas Police Department. When he got an answer he asked for Detective Harold Lacey.

''Where the hell have you been?'' Harry asked, as soon as he heard Wayne's voice. ''Charlene's been worried sick about the both of you. Bobby hasn't called her in over a month.''

''I can't make Bobby telephone his mother,'' Wayne said, grimacing. ''My authority over my deputies only extends so far.''

''Tell Charlene that. She's convinced that all you have to say is 'jump' and Bobby asks 'how far?' ''

''Is she still upset Bobby came to work for me?''

''You know she thinks the world of you,'' Harry said. ''It's just that Bobby's her baby and she didn't want him to move so far away. She still hasn't completely forgiven you for taking off like you did.''

''Well, give her a kiss for me. And tell her Bobby and I will get in touch.''

''You better, or she'll have my hide.'' Harry paused and then asked, ''How's he doing?''

''Bobby?'' Wayne smiled. ''He's coming along fine. He's going to make an excellent officer.''

''Good,'' Harry said gruffly. ''You know I appreciate all you're doing for him.''

''I'm not doing anything more for him than his father did for me.''

Wayne would always be grateful to Harold Lacey. The man had given him something priceless. Belief. Belief in himself. Wayne had been fourteen years old and headed in the wrong direction when Harry had taken him in hand.

"Yeah, well—" Harry sounded embarrassed.

"Listen," Wayne said, knowing Harry was no more comfortable with compliments than he was, "I didn't call you just to get chewed out. That would be a waste of the taxpayers' money."

"So what's up?"

"What have you heard about Stan the Fan Boozer lately?"

"Stan Boozer?" Harry was obviously startled. "Why are you asking me about him? Small-town hoods too tame for you?"

"I saw him today."

"In Crystal Creek? You're kidding."

"With Maynard Kipling."

"You're kidding!"

"Nope. I wouldn't kid about a thing like that."

"Well. Let's see." Harry paused briefly. "You know—come to think of it, Stan and Maynard have been out of Vegas for a while. Maybe they're setting up another branch office."

"In Dallas, for instance? That's where their car was bought."

"Could be. Texas is big on NFL gambling. On any kind of football for that matter. I heard there was even a line on the high school state championships."

"So Boozer is still specializing in football spreads?"

"Yeah. We've tried to nail him, but he's too slick."

"I have someone in town who may be in hock to him."

"Well, I hope he pays his debts. Boozer can play rough."

"Is Boozer still investing in clubs, sports bars, places like that? When I was in the league we had a list of people and places we were supposed to stay away from. Boozer's name was on it."

"As far as we know," Harry answered, "he's still into real estate."

"This guy I mentioned owns a country western dance hall," Wayne said. "It brings in a fair amount of business. You think Boozer would take it in payment?"

"He might. He always was a show business hanger-on. That's where he got his nickname. I heard one time that he dabbled in pirated tapes. Of course, audiotapes are going the way of the LP. Compact discs have made everything else obsolete."

"Why, Harry, you sound upset. Did you have to replace all your Lawrence Welk albums?"

"Hey, watch it. I'm not the one enjoying life in the sticks."

"I have the feeling the sticks might be in for some big-league excitement."

"Good luck if you're right."

"Thanks," Wayne said.

"Remember, you always have a job with the LVPD if the stress gets too much for you."

"I'll remember that."

The two men said their goodbyes and ended the call.

Within fifteen minutes the other two deputies had arrived at the office. When Wayne called the meeting to order, Bobby was still grumbling.

"This had better be good. My first afternoon off in a week, I'm holed up in a cool dark house watching movies with LouAnn Holzer, and Alberta tracks me down and tells me to get my butt over here."

"You better watch out for LouAnn," Gilbert warned Bobby. "She wants to be a cop's wife awfully bad. Ask Wayne. Ask me, for that matter."

"She's never put the make on me," Roy complained.

Everybody laughed.

Gilbert was the first to ask why they'd gathered. "I figure it's something big or you wouldn't have called us in."

"I'm not sure what it is," Wayne said. "But we have to find out. I saw Stan the Fan Boozer and Maynard Kipling coming out of Zack's Place today."

At the varying looks of surprise and bewilderment, Wayne added, "They're big-time gamblers and bookies out of Las Vegas."

"What are they doing in Texas?" Bobby asked. "At Zack's Place, for God's sake."

"That's what I want to know. They might have been out for a ride in the country, but I don't think so," Wayne said. "They might be collecting out-of-the-way honky-tonks. But I don't believe that, either."

"Makes you wonder if Zack's been betting big-time," Gilbert guessed. "Or maybe joined their operation."

"Have you heard any rumors?" Wayne asked him.

"Nothing definite. But I saw Manny Hernandez at Zack's the other day, and we were talking about Manor Downs and a horse he's been treating. Zack came up and wanted some tips. It struck me as odd since Zack never plays the ponies. I don't know—he was acting strange."

"Yeah," Roy said. "I heard he roughed up Jessica Reynolds. Now who'd want to manhandle a pretty lady like that?" Roy remembered something else and glanced warily at his boss.

Wayne took a deep breath. "So far," he said evenly, "all we have is an unexpected visit from two big-league dudes, some odd behavior and Tiny's suspicions."

"What did Tiny say?" Bobby asked.

"That the visit wasn't friendly."

"I'm surprised Tiny was willing to talk to you," Roy said.

"He wasn't really," Wayne said. "Not yet, anyhow. So for now, we'll keep our eyes open and monitor Zack's movements and visitors. If we come up with something, we'll decide what to do. I guarantee you, I won't allow organized gambling in Claro County."

Everyone knew that tone of voice, and the end of the meeting was subdued.

"Gilbert, could you wait outside for a moment?" Wayne asked. "I need to talk to Bobby. Then I'd like to talk to you."

Roy scooted out the door, Gilbert nodded as he left and Bobby's expression changed from eager to worried.

"What's going on?" he asked when they were alone.

"Gilbert was right. LouAnn was persistent. If you're going to bed with her, Bobby, and I wouldn't recommend it, you'd better be using a condom. Because I don't think that's the girl you want to take home to Mom."

Bobby reddened and his look fell away from Wayne's. "I'm taking care of it," he mumbled. "I know what I'm doing."

"Well, however you're doing it, protect yourself." Wayne changed the subject slightly. "I talked to your dad today about Boozer and Kipling. He says Charlene's mad because you haven't written or phoned her. Being an adult means living up to your responsibilities, Bobby. And that includes keeping in touch with your family so they don't worry."

"I know. I know." Bobby looked painfully embarrassed. "I'll call her tonight."

Wayne knew Bobby had a bad case of hero worship and the last thing Wayne wanted to do was humiliate him. "I'm in her bad graces, too. Come by the house tonight and we'll call her together."

"It's a deal." Bobby smiled gratefully and left.

Gilbert came back in and sat down without speaking, waiting for Wayne to explain what he wanted.

"I'd like you to call Austin Vice," Wayne instructed.

"I have an old buddy there. Lenny Greer. He can help us," Gilbert said.

"Find out if he's heard anything about Stan and Maynard. Let him know they've been sighted. Also find out all you can about possible Austin gambling rings. And you might as well ask if APD's had any dealings with Zack. I'm going to have Alberta do a computer check, but I don't think it'll be informative. He can't have anything big on his record or he couldn't have been granted a liquor license."

"Anything else while I'm at it?" Gilbert asked as he got up to leave.

Wayne shook his head. "Nothing for now."

For the next several minutes, Wayne sat at his desk pondering his next action. The problem was he still didn't know enough.

The real problem was he couldn't claim objectivity. Ever since he'd seen Zack's hand twisting Jessie's wrist, Wayne had wanted to break that hand into a hundred pieces.

It wasn't like him to have violent urges. Even on the football field he'd had tight control over his emotions.

Reaching a decision, he made another call. "Mrs. Nelson—this is Wayne Jackson. Is Eugene around?"

"He sure is. You want me to call him to the phone?"

"No. I'd like to come by and talk to him. Is he busy?"

"Busy doing nothing. You come on. Eugene's been underfoot all afternoon."

Chuckling, Wayne said, "I'll be there in a minute."

HE MADE IT IN TEN. The retired sheriff lived on a plot of land abutting the Claro River about a mile outside the town. Unlike Crystal Creek, the river still had water, although it was more than a foot below its usual banks.

Mrs. Nelson met him at the door and pointed the way to the back porch. Wayne found Eugene there in his rocking chair, watching the lackadaisical water and swatting the occasional fly. His dog Cleo lay at his feet.

Eugene pointed Wayne to the companion rocker. "Sit down and rest a spell unless you want to go inside where it's cooler. My bones are so creaky I like the heat."

"This is fine." Wayne took the other rocker.

Eugene spoke first. "So—have you come by to hear me complain about my arthritis? You had to listen to that every day for three years."

Wayne chuckled.

"Or—" Eugene grinned gleefully "—have you come to ask for advice from the old coot?"

"How did you guess?"

"You have that fidgety look. Like you just sat on a burr." Eugene's smile faded as he studied Wayne's expression. "What's bothering you, son?"

"What do you think of Zack Stone?"

After a surprised look, Eugene rocked for a moment. "Well, he's likable enough, if a little slick around the edges. But I can't say I'd trust him with my money or my life."

"Do you think he's capable of big-time racketeering?"

"No."

At Wayne's questioning look, Eugene elaborated. "He hasn't got the stomach for it. Has his betting gotten out of hand?"

"Maybe."

"I told him years ago he'd better keep a lid on it. But there's no point in trying to stop the occasional friendly wager. Don't spend your energy on a shrimp like Zack."

"I have this feeling the shrimp's been swallowed by a barracuda. But I'm not sure I'm being impartial."

"Why?"

Wayne said, "I don't like Zack. I don't like him at all."

"I'm surprised at you, son. You're usually more objective in dealing with people."

"Zack's the exception."

"But why waste your time on him? I've always thought of Zack as essentially harmless."

"Have you ever watched him around a woman?"

"No. I can't say that I have." Eugene eyed Wayne before asking, "Are you talking about a particular woman?"

"Yes."

"Don't tell me you share one."

"No." Wayne was disgusted at the notion.

"I didn't think you went in for the same type. I've heard he enjoys his women flashy. You're more drawn to the homebodies."

"That's right, I am. And that's how I plan to keep it."

"You don't need to persuade me of that."

Snorting, Wayne tried to cover his discomfiture.

"Are you sure this conversation's about Zack Stone at all?" The sly look appeared on Eugene's face again. "Don't tell me you're riled up over some woman. Did you by any chance come by to ask for advice on your love life?"

Wayne gave Eugene a look that didn't need words to express his feelings.

Eugene laughed. "Well, son," he finally said when he could catch his breath, "because you've asked so nice, I'm gonna give you a little."

His expression sobered. "You know, when you came to Crystal Creek, I knew some of your reasons were personal. Hell, I didn't care. I got myself a damn good cop. But I've been watching you ever since, wondering when you would get beyond the bitterness."

"I'm not bitter."

"Call it wary. Comes to the same thing. You've been looking over the women of Crystal Creek like you would a piece of horseflesh."

"That's not wary. That's cold," Wayne protested, not seeing the trap Eugene had laid for him.

"You're right." Eugene snapped the trap shut. "It also makes for cold lonely nights."

Before Wayne could wriggle out, Eugene returned to their original topic. "About Zack—I don't know what you have on him, but I think you owe him the chance to explain. After all, he's been settled here for several years."

"I think you're right," Wayne said after a moment.

"Take someone with you," Eugene suggested, "in case you leave your objectivity behind in the office."

Wayne decided that was probably excellent advice.

CHAPTER FIVE

"JESS, HAVE a listen."

Perched on her stool in the rehearsal studio, Jessie put on her headset and listened intently, beating a rhythm on her thigh. After several minutes she broke into a grin. "It's wonderful, Patrick. That's just the mood I'm aiming for, especially the bluesy wail you added at the chorus." Blowing him a kiss, she said, "You're the best sound man in the business."

"In Austin, at any rate." Patrick didn't pretend modesty. He didn't need to pretend talent. He'd orchestrated and recorded both of Jessie's CDs.

A Nashville studio had been after him, trying to lure him eastward. The West Coast was also beckoning. So far, he'd resisted both offers.

"How long can Austin keep you?" she asked, not sure she wanted to hear his answer.

"Keep me from Nashville or L.A., you mean?" He shook his head dismissively. "They're company towns, Jess. The bottom line's what's important. Here, musicians are closer to their roots. They aren't afraid to risk their careers for their craft."

"But both of us know where the big money gathers."

Patrick shrugged. "If I were interested in big money, that's where I'd gather, too."

She remembered the conversation she'd had with Wayne. "Someone asked me the other day if I planned to leave Austin."

"What did you tell them?"

"Not anytime soon. Although I guess if the right Nashville studio asked me to record for them—" she grinned at Patrick "—and I could persuade you to come with me, I'd probably take the chance."

"I wish I could persuade you to leave Todd Berkley."

"Oh, Patrick. Don't get started on Todd. You'll ruin a perfectly lovely work session."

But Patrick was apparently determined to pursue the subject. "Jess, when are you going to admit you're staying with him out of loyalty?"

"He's kept me in work."

"Barney, the dinosaur, could have kept you in work. You've outgrown Todd. He doesn't have the skills he needs to handle you at this stage of your career. And he knows it."

"He works just as hard for me as he does for the other acts he represents."

"But you're different. And better."

"Don't be silly."

"Jess—look at me."

She did so.

"If you worked in Nashville, I'd move there in a minute."

"Don't say that."

"I mean it. A lot of performers buy their talent in the studio. You bring the talent with you. Remember, I'm the expert."

"Thank you," she said.

"You've created Jessica Reynolds, and she's a class act."

"You make me sound like two different people." But wasn't that exactly what she'd told Wayne?

"All good performers have more than one personality. The trick is finding and using them."

"But what if we use them all up onstage?"

Patrick studied her intently. "Where did that come from? You're not having an attack of self-doubt, are you? Because I can tell you right now these songs we're working on are the best you've written."

Taking his hand, she deflected his question. "I must look like I need encouragement to get your super-duper pep talk."

He turned over his palm and intertwined their fingers. "You look beautiful." He smiled faintly. "But then, what's new?"

Patrick was one of those men who'd wanted to make love to her. As time passed, however, he'd agreed to friendship. For years he'd been a buddy and a sounding board—both personally and professionally. She loved and needed him.

But when he got a certain look—the one he was wearing now—he made her jittery.

"What ideas do you have for that last song I sent you?" she asked, hoping he would follow her change of subject.

He did so. "I want you to sing it so I'll have an idea of the tempo."

This was a song she'd tried first at Zack's the night Wayne had rescued her.

"It's a torch song really," she explained to Patrick. "I sang it with Al and had good audience reaction. I want to work the melody. My voice should dominate. When we record, I'd like the instrumental to be subdued until the end."

With Patrick nodding, she took up her guitar and strummed an introduction. The moment she began the first verse, she was lost in the song.

She felt all the need and desire her phrases conjured. The need she'd experienced when she'd drawn them out of her soul. Singing, she felt alone, yearning for her lover. She ached with the pain of being apart.

When she hit the refrain, her song became a mating call, a cry of hunger. She craved Wayne's touch, his body, his passion....

Stopping abruptly, she swallowed hard and glanced Patrick's way.

He was watching her with a glazed expression. After a moment, he croaked, "Is that all?"

She shook her head nervously.

Sighing deeply, he murmured, "It's more than enough. Honey chile, I'm not sure my equipment can do justice to this one. You almost melted the microphone.

She made a sheepish face. "I tend to get caught up in the words."

With another sigh he muttered, "So do we all."

Patrick shook his head and reverted to his more usual professional manner. "Who do you want to carry the melody, the guitar or the keyboard?"

They began to discuss the best way to achieve the sound she desired.

"Let me fiddle with this, and I'll get back to you," he said, after about twenty minutes.

She nodded, pleased with their preliminary progress. "I have another song," she said impulsively, "that I've just begun. I don't know why, but I can't seem to direct it. The words keep heading off in different directions."

"Maybe I can help."

Again she strummed her guitar and began to sing. "I'd planned my tomorrows....I thought I had options. I didn't know I'd lose you....I thought I could choose...." She stopped, unable to continue past the lump in her throat.

"Why did you decide to write it?" Patrick asked, seeing her distress.

"Because of Dottie's death. I told you about her."

"I hear something besides grief. A kind of searching."

"Well, I—"

Walking into the room, Todd interrupted their talk. "How's it going?" he asked. "Claudia told me you were working."

Claudia was the studio receptionist. She was also a singer in a rock group called the Raunchy Raccoons.

"We were just running through a couple of songs," Jessie said to Todd. "Nothing heavy-duty. I'm still decompressing from our last recording sessions."

"Well, decompress fast because I've got news," he said. "The CD is catching on."

"Where?" she asked skeptically. "In Crystal Creek and Monroe?"

"Sweetheart, you're getting air play all over Texas and Louisiana."

"That's because I've played every dive from here to Baton Rouge."

"Exactly. Everywhere you've gone, your sales are out of sight. And this new CD has legs." He pointed to Patrick. "You did a good job with this one, ol' buddy."

Patrick pointed at him mockingly. "Jess had something to do with it, too—ol' buddy."

Todd gestured expansively. "Of course she did. And we've got to get her back out there before a wider public."

She asked, "What have I been doing all these years?"

"Playing dives—like you said. I'm starting to look at bigger, uptown venues. And I think we're ready for a nationwide tour."

"Better to build up a regional following before you tackle the entire U.S. market," Patrick advised him.

Todd turned his way indignantly. "Are you trying to tell me how to run Jessie's career?"

Before Patrick could elaborate, Jessie stepped in. "What do you mean, nationwide, Todd?"

"We'll start in the South. Then see if we can pick up some dates in California."

"How long do you plan for me to stay on the road?"

"Three months—four—six. Whatever it takes?"

She could tell by Todd's exasperated sigh that her expression was less than enthusiastic.

"Now, Jessie," he said. "We've already hashed this out. The road's where it's at for an unknown performer. Besides, it's not like you're leaving anyone behind."

"Only my life," she said a little wearily.

"Your career's your life. At least, that's what you've told me. Has that changed?"

"No, no, it hasn't changed."

"Don't you like going out and making new fans?"

"Yes, of course, I do." And that was the part of touring that still excited her, that made the long hours on the highway worth it. Standing in front of an unfamiliar audience, knowing it was up to her to win them over. The thrill of accomplishment when she knew she'd succeeded.

"Listen, Jessie—" Todd's voice called her back from her thoughts. "I'll work my butt off putting together this tour. The least you can do is be enthusiastic."

"Back off, Todd." Patrick's expression grew ominous. "Jess has a right to a little stability and privacy."

"You back off, Patrick." Todd turned on him. "Who says she can't have a private life on the road?" He grinned knowingly. "Most of us manage it."

Patrick snorted with disgust.

Jessie tried to intervene, but both men ignored her.

"I'm not the bad guy here, you know," Todd said. "I'm slaving for this woman."

"You're slaving to squeeze as much money out of her as you can."

Todd held out his hands in elaborate bewilderment. "For us all. I'm working to make money for us all."

"Jess is making the money. It's her talent you're peddling. And there are others who can peddle it for her a damn sight better."

Todd blew up. "I'm a damned good agent! As good as anyone you'd find on either coast."

Jessie had had all she could take. "Okay. Okay. That's enough." She had to literally step between the combatants. Twisting around to Todd, she said, "Of course I'll go on an extended tour."

"I'm telling you, Jessie, this will be the best thing for your career." Ignoring Patrick, Todd took hold of Jessie's hand. "I know what I'm talking about. This CD is hot. It's fresh. You're this close to the big leagues—" Todd measured the air with his thumb and forefinger. "Only you've got to do your part. That's why you've got to rethink this problem you have with appearing at Zack's."

"I told you I wouldn't do it."

"The contract's iron-clad."

"You've gotten me out of contracts before."

"Only when the other party was willing."

Jessie made a sound of frustration. "I warned you Zack might give you trouble. But I asked you to hold firm."

"Sweetheart—Zack's hurt by your attitude. He reminded me that he's done a lot for you over the years."

"I know, but—"

"We don't want to end up on his bad side," Todd cautioned. "He draws a lot of area customers and people in the business."

She glanced Patrick's way. Didn't Todd realize this kind of discussion only strengthened Patrick's dislike of him? But, then, Todd could be amazingly myopic.

"Todd, Zack made moves on me."

"Lots of men move in on you."

"I couldn't seem to discourage him."

"Oh, come on, Jessie, I can't believe that. I've seen you say no to a man and make him believe it. You warned Patrick and me off clear enough."

"Don't bring my name into this," Patrick growled.

"I'm just don't understand why Zack's different," Todd said, glaring. "Unless maybe she's sending him mixed signals."

His words threw Jessie off balance. It was true she did sometimes worry that her sexy onstage persona confused her needier customers. Which was another reason she dressed simply when she wasn't performing.

"Jessie doesn't send mixed signals," Patrick said. "At least, not the way you mean," he blurted out.

"What way do *you* mean?" she asked, startled.

Clearly uncomfortable, Patrick searched for words. "You're just so damned tempting," he finally said. "Like you were a while ago when you were singing. You rush a man's senses."

The way she had Wayne's? He'd found her tempting but dangerous. Too dangerous. Could she be one of those women who were bad for a man?

Feeling defeated, she asked Todd, "How many gigs do I have left at Zack's?"

"Only one more, sweetheart. Then I promise you'll never have to appear there again. Or else you'll be so big you can hire your own bodyguards."

The image made Jessie queasy, but it reminded her that Tiny would be there to protect her. "Okay," she said to end the argument.

"You won't regret this," Todd said.

"But you're to tell Zack I find his advances objectionable, and I will leave and not come back if he tries anything else."

"Absolutely," Todd said.

With her capitulation, Patrick stalked away, muttering.

Todd, however, was as pleased as punch.

IT WAS SUNDAY AFTERNOON and Wayne and Gilbert were out in one of the department vehicles. Gilbert was driving, and Wayne sat in the passenger seat, restless with the task ahead.

"So Lenny, your friend in Vice, couldn't give you much on Zack?" he asked. "Had APD ever had any contact with him?"

"Oh, yes. But only in the past. Apparently Zack's been around the music scene since he was a university student. He even played in a country western band. He's been pulled in on minor charges—traffic tickets, that sort of thing. He was suspected of dealing pot, nickel and diming it. But nothing since he moved to Crystal Creek. Actually, Lenny was surprised to hear from me. He thought Zack had given up his wild youth and discovered capitalistic respectability."

"I think he had," Wayne said. "Until recently. What did Lenny say when you told him about Stanley and Maynard?"

"He was most perturbed."

"Does he have any idea of why they're here?"

"As he pointed out, illegal gambling is a big growth industry in Texas. He thinks Kipling and Boozer have moved in to claim their share of the take."

"That's what I believe," Wayne said somberly. "I hate to see it happening. On-track betting and lotto have only fueled people's fantasies."

"Spoken like a true officer of the law." Gilbert smiled.

"After you've been in Vegas and seen what gambling can do to people, it's hard to think of it as anything but an addiction."

"I suppose so," Gilbert said, sounding subdued.

"I didn't mean to lecture," Wayne offered by way of an apology. "My ex-wife's a compulsive gambler."

"I didn't know." Gilbert glanced Wayne's way as if waiting for a cue.

When Wayne remained silent, Gilbert continued with his narrative. "Anyway—APD asked us to give them anything we could on Kipling and Boozer. I said we'd get back with them as soon as we'd seen Zack."

"Not that I think this afternoon will be particularly enlightening," Wayne said.

"Oh—" Gilbert remembered "—Lenny also asked us to help them."

"How?"

"Austin's being flooded with pirated videos. They're beginning to think it's a distribution center for the whole Southwest. They're convinced the copying operation is local. They asked us to be on the lookout."

Pirated tapes...where had Wayne heard that phrase recently?

"You told Lenny we hadn't seen anything suspicious other than Boozer and Kipling," Wayne said.

"Yes, boss."

Gilbert pulled into the parking lot of Zack's Place. The club was closed, but Zack's car was one of two parked around back so they knew he should be in the building.

Wayne and Gilbert went directly to the back door. After Gilbert had knocked loudly for several seconds, they heard Zack's voice.

"We're closed," he said. "Come back tomorrow."

"It's Sheriff Jackson and Deputy Rodriguez," Wayne called. "We need to talk to you."

Silence greeted his announcement. Several seconds passed before Zack's voice trickled out the door.

"Why? We haven't called about any trouble."

The two officers moved cautiously to either side of the entrance. "Open the door, Zack. We have to talk."

Zack did as he was bidden with obvious reluctance. Blinking against the light, he looked a little pale. When he tried to close the door behind him, Wayne pushed it open.

"I think we'll go inside," he said, "where it's cool."

There was fear all around. Wayne could smell it in the air.

Ushering Zack to his office, Wayne waited for Gilbert to follow. "Whose is that other car?" Wayne asked in the meantime.

"It's Tom, the bartender's," Zack said quickly. "It wouldn't start last night, and he hasn't returned to tow it."

"So you're the only one in the building?"

"Yes."

Gilbert came in just then and nodded agreement. "I checked the dance hall. I didn't see anybody."

"What do you mean?" Zack asked, his jaw jutting forward. "You don't have the right to search my place. You don't have a warrant."

"We were just curious to see if you were alone."

"I come here most Sundays to check the week's take. What's all this about, Sheriff? I haven't done anything."

"Then there's no reason for you to be defensive," Wayne said.

"I'm not so sure. After last week when you pushed me around—"

That remark drew a glance from Gilbert.

"I considered calling Martin Avery," Zack continued, "or one of the city council. But I knew I wouldn't get any justice. You're pretty much king of the hill around here."

"Feel free to complain to whoever you want to."

Again, Gilbert glanced his way in surprise.

"Since Ms. Reynolds won't be appearing here again, I consider what happened last week a closed chapter," Wayne said.

Zack's expression flickered.

"What?" Wayne asked immediately.

"Nothing," Zack said.

"We're here on a different matter," Wayne went on, watching Zack closely. "What do you know about Stan the Fan Boozer and Maynard Kipling?"

Zack's face froze. "I—I've never heard of them," he finally got out.

"You're a lousy liar," Wayne said.

"I'm not lying."

"We're here to help," Gilbert said, "if you'll let us."

"Why would I need help?" Zack sounded a little wild.

Tiny was right, Zack's control was iffy.

"If you were up to your ears in gambling debts..." Wayne's voice trailed off.

"What have you heard—? I don't owe anybody. Oh—well—maybe a C note here or there. But I'm good for that. You can ask anybody."

"Stan the Fan is one of the biggest gamblers in the country," Wayne said. "We saw him and his side-kick coming out of here two days ago. You're a football fan. Are you trying to tell me you don't know one of the heaviest odds makers around?"

"Is that who those two guys were?" Zack said feebly. "I thought they looked out of place."

"In your office?" Wayne asked. "Doesn't sound like they were casual customers."

"Who's been talking?"

"Don't you know you can't hide anything in these parts?"

Zack's face grew belligerent. "Especially when the sheriff is out to get you."

"Why would you think that?" Gilbert asked.

"Because we've got our eye on the same woman." Zack flashed a look Wayne's way. "I heard how you took Jessie home and chauffeured her around the day of Dottie's funeral. I heard about the big clinch in the church parking lot."

"Zack," Wayne said gently, "if I find out you have your eyes or anything else on Ms. Reynolds again, I will come after you."

Gesturing to Wayne, Zack said, "You heard him threaten me, Rodriguez."

"I heard him caution you about sexual harassment," Gilbert said.

"See what I mean? I knew I couldn't get a fair shake around here." Resentment was replaced by a calculating look. "That's okay, Sheriff. You may be able to push me around, but don't think your badge will get you into Jessie's panties. She's gotten real picky about who she takes to her bed."

When Wayne started toward Zack, Gilbert put out a cautionary hand, and took over the questioning. "We're very concerned with Boozer and Kipling's business with you. Can you clear the meeting up for us?"

"I told you they were customers. Nothing else."

"Don't be stupid about this," Gilbert cautioned. "You've been taking football bets for years. We could bring charges and produce witnesses. You'd lose your liquor license. Without booze, Zack's Place would die."

By this time, Wayne had calmed down enough to turn and study the effect Gilbert's predictions had on Zack.

Even in the dim light, his pale face seemed to whiten further. "I've brought revenue to this town. I've kept my nose clean. I've built up the business. This is all I have."

His look met Wayne's. "If you hadn't—" He caught himself. "You have it in for me because of Jessie. Everything was fine until the other night."

"The other night has nothing to do with the information we're requesting," Wayne said. "All you have to do is come clean about Boozer and Kipling.

If you owe them money, we can deal with that. But I won't have gambling rackets in Claro County. If you obstruct our investigation, you'll lose in every way."

"I don't have to listen to this. You know your way out."

"You're making a big mistake," Gilbert said. "If you're scared of what they'll do, your best protection is to cooperate with us."

"I don't need protection. Except from him." Zack gestured in Wayne's direction.

Wayne had had all he could take of Zack's whining. "You will need protection if you bother Ms. Reynolds in the future. Remember that."

Zack flinched at Wayne's warning, but his mouth remained stubbornly closed.

Disgusted, Wayne swung around and left. He was standing by the car staring into the distance when Gilbert caught up with him.

Both men were quiet as they began the journey into town.

"I should have filled you in on my earlier brush with Zack," Wayne said finally.

"It would have helped. Although I saw soon enough what was between you."

What had he seen? Wayne wondered, trying to view the scene just past through Gilbert's eyes.

"I gather Jessie Reynolds is going to be a complication," Gilbert said.

"She has nothing to do with this," Wayne objected.

Gilbert glanced over at him before saying mildly, "I've never seen you lose your cool before, boss."

"If you could have watched while he smeared his hands over her—" Wayne realized how he sounded and abruptly stopped. Clearing his throat, he began again. "You're right, I did lose my cool. That's why I wanted you with me. Am I right? Did I smell fear back there?"

"He's scared as hell," Gilbert agreed. "And I'll tell you something else. He wasn't alone in the building. I saw the blinds twitch in one of those back rooms as I came out. Now why would Zack lie about that?"

"Good question."

Both men retreated into their thoughts.

Wayne found his particularly galling. He'd made a fool of himself a moment ago. Worse, he'd committed errors in judgment. Stupid errors that in another context could have cost him and his deputy. He had to somehow regain control.

Only he wasn't sure how to do that. He'd thought he could put danger behind him. He'd assumed his life would return to normal without Jessie's presence to torment him.

Instead, he'd been tempted to tear a suspect limb from limb for mentioning her name.

He'd gotten her out of his life, but what good had it done him? He was becoming obsessed with every memory he had of her.

So few memories, each so vivid. The way she walked, her husky voice, her disconcerting honesty. The feel of her body under his hands.

Wayne looked down and realized his palms had just skimmed his thighs in frustration. When he looked over at Gilbert, he found the other man staring.

"Wayne," Gilbert said after a moment, "don't keep me in the dark on this case. Is there something I should know?"

Wayne shook his head wearily. "There's nothing to tell you."

"So Zack was just talking when he said—?"

"I've spoken to the lady on three different occasions. And I helped her at the funeral because she'd been torn up at Dottie's death. I haven't seen her since. There's nothing between us. I doubt that I'll ever see Jessica Reynolds again."

CHAPTER SIX

THE AUSTIN NEIGHBORHOOD where Jessie's garage apartment was located had seen better times. However, today as always, Jessie enjoyed the drive home. The streets were wide and tree-lined, and many of the homes were gingerbread Victorian.

It was late afternoon, and a thunderstorm had washed away the heat of the day. The twilight promised a lazy summer night, perfect for lawn chair philosophizing. Maybe she'd give Patrick a call and invite him over for supper and a beer. She and he had spent many an evening on her front stoop discussing life, art and country western music. Only this evening he'd have to promise not to argue with her about Todd. She wasn't up to arguing.

She'd spent today—her day off from Kickers—cleaning her nest. She'd been bustling around since early this morning, armed with a mop, a broom, rags and various odoriferous cleansers, along with the restlessness that comes after a troubled night.

If she couldn't get her life in order, at least she could organize her overflowing closet. If she couldn't wipe out these past few weeks, she could at least wipe away the layer of dust that had accumulated over her secondhand furniture. If she couldn't see what the future held, she could at least wash her windows in order to enjoy the view of her landlady's leafy garden.

Mrs. Peters, her landlady, was out inspecting her lawn when Jessie pulled up in the driveway with the groceries. A widow who'd lived in the same house for decades, she had added the apartment as an income provider when her husband died.

A staid, old-fashioned soul, Mrs. Peters had been doubtful about Jessie's vocation. But the two women had long since become neighborly, and Jessie let her know whenever she left on tour. She was glad for someone who knew her out-of-town schedule and could look after her belongings when she was on the road.

Seeing her tenant arrive, Mrs. Peters called out to her, "I was just checking the grass to decide whether I should water. I think we got enough rain this time to soak the ground."

"Looks that way," Jessie came back. "Isn't this break in the weather great?"

"Maybe we'll have an early autumn."

"I hope so." Jessie grabbed sacks of food and hauled them up the stairs.

She made a second trip and was headed back out the screen door for a final foray when she found Zack on her stoop, holding detergent and a six-pack—her last two items.

Instinctively, her eyes searched the yard, but Mrs. Peters had gone inside.

"I thought you might like help with this," Zack said, offering his load.

Jessie took it from him without yielding any space. "What are you doing here?" she asked.

"I thought you wouldn't mind if we had a talk." His tone was obsequious, his face the picture of affability.

"I need to put my groceries away."

"I'll come inside and watch."

"I'd rather you didn't."

His expression turned woeful. "Hey—aren't you ever going to forgive me for the other night?"

"You haven't asked for forgiveness. You haven't even apologized."

Opening his arms wide, he asked, "Why do you think I'm here?"

She leaned against the door jamb, still suspicious. "Why *are* you here?"

"To say I'm sorry."

"I'm not sure I believe you."

"I promise it's true. Honest, Jessie, I feel bad about what happened. You were absolutely right. I stepped way out of line. I thought since we'd dated a few times—"

"You thought wrong. We never dated. And you stepped *way* out of line. It wasn't the first time, but it had better be the last. I guess Todd told you to come here."

"Why would Todd do that?" Zack asked, his bewilderment genuine.

"Haven't you talked to him about my contract?"

"Yes. And I really appreciate your sticking to it. You're one of my best draws."

"Did Todd tell you to keep your hands to yourself?"

For the briefest moment, Zack's face turned ugly. In fact, Jessie wasn't even sure she'd seen the flash of anger.

Especially when Zack laughed heartily. "He sure did. That manager of yours is looking out for you. I heard what he said, and I hear what you're saying, and I understand. I hope you'll let bygones be bygones."

"Okay, I will," Jessie said and smiled briefly. "Thanks for the apology, Zack. Goodbye."

Zack caught her wrist when she turned to go inside. She twisted back around, her eyes blazing.

He loosened his grip. "I'm sorry. I'm sorry." Backing away, he almost fell down the stairs.

This time she caught him and pulled him to safety. Then something about the situation struck her as funny. She started laughing. A second later, Zack joined in.

"See, Jessie," he said after a moment, "I just want us to be friends. We go back a ways, kid. We've shared a lot of laughs. I'd hate to lose you."

It was true. Jessie had known Zack since before he opened Zack's Place. Once he'd even been after her to sing with a band he'd put together.

Studying him now, she saw the Zack of old. A little slick around the edges, perhaps a little too eager, but generous, a good buddy and certainly manageable.

"You're right." She patted his arm where she'd earlier grabbed him. "Apology accepted." She held out her hand.

He shook it but only briefly, as if to show her he meant to keep his distance.

"Hadn't you better put your groceries away?" he asked.

"Yes." She glanced down into the yard before giving Zack a penetrating look. His familiar expression reassured her. "Come on in. You want a beer?"

"Sure do." He followed her inside, maintaining his casual air. When she went into the kitchen, he stayed in the living room.

"Todd says your CD's jumping off the shelves," he said.

From out of a sack, Jessie took lettuce and celery. "That's what he told me."

"It won't be long before you'll be too expensive for Zack's Place."

"I hope so," she said from the depths of the refrigerator.

He groaned. "Is that any way to talk to the worried owner?"

She straightened. "Why worried?"

"Oh—" He hemmed and hawed for a moment. "Crystal Creek's not a very friendly place anymore."

She came out of the kitchen curious at his tone. "Why's that?"

He shrugged. "Different reasons. I'm not Sheriff Jackson's favorite person these days. I think it's because of you."

"What do I have to do with anything?" The direction of the conversation was unexpected. But she realized in a flash why Zack was here.

"Rumor has it," Zack said, "that you and the sheriff are friendly."

"Friendly?" she repeated, trying to contain her alarm.

"Somebody saw you kissing. Said you were steaming up his windows."

"That's ridiculous." Jessie could feel her face flame.

"Maybe so." Zack shrugged again. "But I was worried that maybe he'd taken it personally when I came on to you."

"The sheriff and I met for the first time that night. How could he take it personally? Don't you remember him introducing himself?"

"Yeah. But some things start fast. I heard he took you home later and stayed awhile." There was a hint of prurience beneath Zack's ingenuous air.

"That was because of Dottie," Jessie said brusquely.

"Yeah. I heard he escorted you around the day of her funeral."

Jessie had had enough of Zack and his rumors. She crossed her arms and faced him directly. "Just what is this about?"

"Don't get upset with me. I'm only relaying what people are saying."

"Maybe so. But why did you feel it was important enough to drive all the way to Austin to tell me about it?"

"Well, I . . . I wondered if maybe—since you have an in with the sheriff—you could put in a good word for me."

Jessie wasn't sure what she'd been bracing herself for. Certainly not this strange request.

"Zack, that's about the craziest thing you've ever asked me to do," she said. "In the first place, the sheriff and I aren't involved, no matter what people are saying. And if we were, I'd never interfere with his work. He seems a fair enough man."

"I'm telling you he's out to get me," Zack muttered, avoiding her gaze.

"Well, I'm sorry," she said reasonably. "But it has nothing to do with me."

"Come on, I'm no fool. I have eyes and ears like anybody else."

"I'm not sure what you're saying, but I think it's time you—"

"Every time I mention you he tries to tear me to pieces."

"Does he? Then don't mention me." Jessie tried to hide her trembling.

"I'm telling you, Jessie. You owe me one. You got me into this mess."

"What mess?" she asked, mystified. "I still don't know why you're so upset. Okay—so Wayne doesn't like you. If you've broken no laws then it doesn't matter."

"Everybody breaks the law these days," Zack mumbled.

"Then maybe what you need is an attorney," she said.

"I've been gambling." He eyed the floor. "I owe a little too much to some people from Dallas."

"I'm sorry to hear that. You know—people have been warning you for years you needed to cut down. Maybe you ought to listen to your friends for a change."

"I am. I am. But I don't need Sheriff Jackson breathing down my neck while I straighten things out. Listen—everything I have is sunk into Zack's Place. You and I go back a long way, kid," he reminded her again. "I gave you a few breaks when you needed them."

"I know that." She nodded. "And I'll always be grateful."

"So, now I'm telling you, Jessie, I need a break."

"I can't help you," she said, distressed at his agitation. "I'm sorry, Zack. If I could, I would."

"Yeah, sure." His face darkened with anger. "Always ready to help your fellow man—when it suits you. Well, listen, if you know what's good for you, you'll come through for me."

With his thinly veiled threat, her compassion faded. "That's enough. I've said I can't help you. I think you'd better leave."

She sidestepped him to open the door, and he grabbed at her. Before she could react, however, he dropped his hands and backed away.

"I'm sorry. I didn't mean it." He hurried outside. "I just— I just thought you could help. My mistake. We'll forget it."

"It certainly was your mistake." Jessie latched the screen against him. "I'm sorry you're having trouble with Sheriff Jackson, but if you threaten me again, I'll call the police."

Again, his expression flared for the briefest moment before he turned and descended the stairs.

She leaned against the door, feeling suddenly weak, and tried to assure herself that the threat Zack had made was merely bravado. The rest of the time, she remembered, he'd labored to appear ingratiating. And it was true he had the right to press her for a favor. So why was she left with the taste of fear in her mouth?

Zack had changed somehow in the past few weeks. His self-control was unreliable. Murky depths were beginning to bubble up over the practiced charm.

Wayne was the motivation for Zack's visit. She should call him. She wanted to call him. She needed to call him to tell him . . . to hear his voice. . . .

But he didn't want to hear her or see her or touch her or hold her.

Sinking down on the couch, she worked to slow her breathing, trying to push away the images that had been haunting her for a week.

She was beginning to think she'd lost her mind completely. She'd certainly lost her reason along with her caution and what little intelligence she could claim. Letting Zack inside had been stupid. She should have gone with her initial caution. She decided she could use some expert advice.

Picking up the phone, she opened her directory, found a number and dialed it.

"Austin Police Department."

"Is Lenny Greer on duty? He works in Vice."

"Could you hold? I'll connect you."

"Thank you."

After a moment, Greer came on the line.

"Lenny, this is Jessie. Jessica Reynolds."

"Well, hello, Jessie. How's my favorite guardian angel?"

"Don't start that again. That's not why I called."

"Can I help it if I have a soft spot in my heart for the woman who saved my life?"

"All I did was stem the bleeding until the ambulance arrived."

"I'll never forget your face hovering above me. I thought I'd died and gone to heaven."

She laughed. "And all the time you were spread-eagled in the sawdust at Kickers—"

"With a bullet hole in my side where the SOB shot me."

"Well, you were about to arrest him for procuring. Anyway, look on the bright side. After he took a shot at you, he was up for attempted murder."

"And your testimony helped convict him. You *are* an angel." He swung into song. "Wanna date with an angellll. Wanna meet her at seveennn." His voice dipped lower. "How about it, Jessie?"

"Now, Lenny—"

"Okay, okay." He sighed. "I had to try. To what do I owe this unexpected pleasure?"

"I need some advice."

"Let's hear it."

"A man just threatened me," she said.

Lenny became all business. "Are you calling to report this, because I'll need to bring in someone from a different department."

"Well, it wasn't much of a threat," she hedged. "That's why I wanted to talk to you unofficially. I was appearing at his club about a week ago and after one of the shows he put the make on me. When I tried to discourage him, he wouldn't listen. Someone had to step in and pull him away."

"Do you want to press charges?"

"That didn't happen in Austin. Besides, I don't have anything really to charge him with. Today, when he came by my apartment, he was a perfect gentleman, except he wanted me to do him a favor. When I said I couldn't, he said if I knew what was good for me, I'd do what he asked. Are you following me so far?"

"Yes."

"I guess I wanted you to tell me what to do if he ever pulls something like this again."

"If he threatens you again, you contact us immediately. With this new stalking law the legislature's passed, we can charge him with harassing you. If you want, we could have a talk with him now so that he knows you mean business."

"He doesn't live in Austin, he lives in Crystal Creek."

"Who exactly are you talking about?" Lenny asked again, his voice sharpening.

"Just a guy who owns a dance hall. I've appeared there before. But he's changed— I don't know—"

"Are you talking about Zack Stone?" Lenny interrupted.

"How did you know?"

"Lucky guess," he said dryly. "Shouldn't you tell Sheriff Jackson about this?"

She didn't think to ask why Wayne's name came up so readily. She only knew it made her uneasy. "No, no—I don't want to bother him. He was the one who stepped in when Zack came on too strong. Besides, Zack was in Austin today. Out of Way— I mean Sheriff Jackson's jurisdiction."

"I still think you'd better fill him in. He's interested in Zack."

"Look, it's not important. I just wanted to investigate my options. If he bothers me again, you'll be the first to know."

"Okay, but I might want to talk to you later about this."

Now why would Lenny need to do a thing like that? Jessie thought better of asking the question. "Anyway," she said, "thanks for the advice." She chuckled. "And the sweet talk."

"Where are you singing these days?" he asked abruptly.

"I'm back at Kickers for the time being."

"You'll be there tonight?"

"Tomorrow."

"Save a seat for me, I might drop in."

He'd come to hear her before, so why did she have a strange feeling about his request? She managed a joking comeback, however. "If you do, you might want to wear a bulletproof vest."

WAYNE WAS on autopilot when he hit the city limits. A few nagging thoughts had preoccupied his mind during the drive—some possibilities he wanted to discuss with the Austin police.

He could have sent Gilbert to this impromptu meeting, but he'd decided he wanted to meet Lenny Greer in person, if that were possible. It paid to cultivate contacts in the law enforcement business. Nothing accomplished that like the personal touch.

Besides, he had to give himself some reason why he'd driven forty miles on a potential wild-goose chase.

He'd been to Austin police headquarters before, and this evening he found his way without any problem. If Wayne was lucky, he'd be able to track Greer down. If not, he'd discuss developments with whoever was on duty.

He was more than lucky. Greer was at his desk and surprisingly pleased to meet Wayne.

After the introductions, Lenny offered a chair. "Have a seat. I think we have things to discuss."

"That's why I came to town," Wayne said. "I hoped I could be of help to you." He got right down to business. "In the past week, I've heard piracy mentioned twice. Once in regard to audiotapes, the second, regarding videos, came from your office."

"How did you hear about piracy the first time?"

"From one of my buddies at the Las Vegas Police Department. I used to work there. I spoke to him about our friends Stanley and Maynard. According to LVPD, they've been suspected in the past of audiotape piracy. Sort of a sideline business before CDs got so big. Which made me wonder—"

"If maybe they'd branched out again."

"In Central Texas."

Lenny looked thoughtful. "Well, it's worth some follow-up. Whoever's doing this has access to mint-condition videos. That means they have connections within the distribution industry. If Boozer and Kipling already had contacts, it would be relatively simple to change technologies. I'll look into it right away."

"In the meantime, I'm keeping an eye on Zack's Place. My gut feeling is he knows something or is somehow involved. He didn't much want to see us last Sunday."

"Speaking of Zack—he's popped up in Austin."

"Oh? Gilbert said you hadn't heard from him recently."

"It seems he paid a visit to Jessica Reynolds yesterday. Crowded her a little, then backed off."

Wayne's face stilled. "What do you mean 'crowded her'?"

"Said she owed him a favor. That she'd be sorry if she didn't come through."

"What sort of favor?" Wayne's voice was deadly quiet.

"She didn't tell me."

"Well, she'll damn well tell me."

Catching sight of Lenny's expression, Wayne realized he'd lost his cool. He waited for Lenny to continue.

"Don't worry, he left without harming her. The only reason she phoned me was to get some advice."

"I'll give her some advice." Wayne stood. "She should have called me."

Lenny agreed matter-of-factly. "I thought so myself. In fact I suggested she do so."

"And what did she say?"

"She didn't seem to like the idea."

Growling, Wayne started toward the exit before swinging around to face Lenny. "Why did she call you? Do you know each other?"

"I met her on an investigation. She was one of our star witnesses."

Before Wayne could question him further, Lenny said soothingly, "I assure you there's nothing but friendship between us. She came to my rescue, we got to be friends, and I've told her to call me anytime she needed to."

"What do you mean, came to your rescue?"

"I was lying on the floor of Kickers bleeding profusely. She applied a pressure tourniquet. Possibly saved my life."

"Oh. I see. Yeah, I see what you mean."

Wayne felt sheepish and tried to regain his dignity. "Listen, who Jessie's friends with is none of my business." He changed the subject. "Are you sure she's not in danger?"

For the first time, Lenny's voice was cool. "She didn't seem to think Zack posed a threat to her. She just wanted to know how to handle him if he harassed her again."

Wayne said, "It won't happen again."

"I can believe that," Lenny murmured.

His remark brought a thin smile to Wayne's lips. "Sorry," he said. "I didn't mean to come on so strong. I'm driving over to Kickers. You want to come along?"

"No," Lenny said, drawing out the word. "I think I'd just as soon stay out of the fray. Let me know if you learn anything pertinent to our inquiry. And Wayne—let me know if you think Jessie needs protection."

"I'll do that," Wayne said, then was gone.

ALL DURING THE SET Jessie felt as if someone was staring at her. She also felt foolish since, of course, someone *was* staring—a room full of someones who'd paid for the privilege.

Stage fright wasn't usually a problem once she began her performance. Once she began, the music always took hold of her, carrying her and her audience to a private place they shared.

Except the feelings tonight weren't the remnants of stage fright. She wasn't sure she could identify what caused them. Only that she couldn't remember ever having felt them before.

She wasn't particularly happy to find Todd waiting for her outside her dressing room together with Claudia, the studio receptionist.

Jessie summoned a smile for her visitors. Maybe it was Claudia's gimlet gaze she'd sensed earlier. The two women were more rivals than friends.

Todd, however, was his usual enthusiastic self. "You were great, as always." He bussed Jessie's cheek. "I love that new torch song. You had the men drooling."

Todd had such powers of language.

"And all the women wishing they were you," he added.

"Not *all* the women." Claudia pouted.

Jessie sat down before her mirror and began to touch up her makeup. She had thirty minutes before her next performance. *Please,* she prayed silently, *let a few of them be solitary.*

"What brings you here tonight?" she asked.

"I hadn't caught your act in a while," Todd said. "Figured I might have some helpful hints for you. You leave pretty soon on the minitour I set up."

"I know," she said, repressing a sigh.

"Now, sweetheart, we need more enthusiasm. A couple of times during the set I thought you lost your pizzazz. An audience senses that."

"I know."

There was a knock on the door. Jessie called for the visitor to enter. One of the waiters came in with a glass of chipped ice and a bottle of sparkling water, Jessie's only standing request.

"Anything else I can get for you, Ms. Reynolds?" he asked, while he placed the drink and ice beside her and filled the glass.

She didn't usually eat between performances. Adrenaline worked best with an empty stomach. But

for some reason, her stomach had giant butterflies
fluttering inside. Another ominous sign?

She turned to the waiter. "Do you have any
soup?"

"Vegetable."

"I'd like a bowl with crackers."

The waiter nodded. "Coming right up."

As he was leaving, Todd looked at her questioningly.

"You know food slows you down," he said as
though enlightening her.

"I know."

"Hey—what is this?" He gestured dismay. "Cat
got your tongue? 'I know,' 'I know.' Is that all
you've got for me? Are you still mad about Zack and
your contract? Because believe me, Jessie, you did
the smart thing."

"Ah, hell," she muttered, swinging her legs back
around so that she gazed at the mirror. She made a
face at her reflection. It only took this to cap a perfect night.

"Zack came by my apartment yesterday," she
said. "He was pretty obnoxious."

"Did he try anything?"

"No."

"Well, then?"

"I think you'd better have another talk—"

A second knock interrupted her. The waiter must
have gone out of his way to fill her order so quickly.

She took a sip from her drink and called, "Come in." Smiling into the mirror, she waited to thank his reflection.

Instead, when the door opened, the figure that loomed in the shadows of the hall was not the waiter.

CHAPTER SEVEN

JESSIE'S SMILE FROZE. Her heart began clamoring. The ice in her glass rattled in her grip before she carefully placed it beside her makeup tray.

Todd started toward the shadowy intruder. "I'm sorry," he said, "but Ms. Reynolds doesn't see anyone until after her last set."

Wayne brushed by Todd as though he weren't there.

"Why didn't you call me after Zack threatened you?" Wayne's tone was imperative as he advanced upon her.

"You said you didn't want to hear from me."

"That was personal. This—"

"Now wait a minute." Todd scurried to her side. "I said visitors weren't allowed. You'd better leave."

He might have been a buzzing mosquito for all the attention Wayne paid him.

Jessie, reluctant to see Todd a splat on the wall, intervened. "Todd, this is Sheriff Jackson from Crystal Creek. He's here on business. The episode with Zack."

By this time, Todd had assimilated the proportions of his opponent. "What can we do for you, Sheriff?" he asked, considerably more docile.

Continuing to ignore him, Wayne leaned against the dressing table so that his thigh brushed Jessie's arm. "Why wouldn't you call me?" he repeated.

"Sheriff Jackson," she said, trying not to sound winded, "this is my agent, Todd Berkley. And his friend, Claudia Broussard."

Claudia sidled over, encompassing him with a single look. "What a shame you're a cop," she murmured, testing his biceps.

Without a change in expression, Wayne stared down at her fingers. After a second, Claudia dropped her hand.

"I was just telling Todd about yesterday when you came in," Jessie said, wading into the silence.

Wayne waited.

"Zack didn't exactly threaten me," she explained painstakingly. "He wanted a favor. It had to do with you."

Her gaze met Wayne's. The air between them crackled. They might as well have been the only people in the room.

"He thought the two of us had something going. Isn't that silly? He wanted me to intercede with you on his behalf. He says he's managed to get on your bad side." Somehow her speech had given her courage. Her speech and his nearness. Enough courage to murmur, "As if you had one."

A reluctant smile conquered his lips. He banished it before it took over his features. His look narrowed. "Don't think," he said, "that you'll slip out of this easily. You told me you'd report if Zack got out of line."

Her gaze fell to her entwined fingers. "I wasn't sure which of your instructions I should follow. You were pretty specific that last day."

"Leave that day out of it. Did Zack say why I'm after him?"

"He said he owes gambling debts and is trying to make good on them. But he says it'll be hard to do that with you breathing down his neck. I told him to go to you. I told him you'd impressed me as a fair and impartial man." She glanced at him from under her lashes. "Maybe I fudged on that one."

"Why does Zack feel like you owe him a favor?" Wayne asked ignoring her comment.

"He's given me a break or two. He's been a generous employer."

"Well, right now he can't afford to be generous. He's in a tight spot. And desperate men can turn dangerous. How did he threaten you?"

"He just said that if I knew what was good for me, I'd help him out. And he could, if he wanted to, make my life difficult. He knows quite a few people involved in the music scene. But he didn't sound dangerous." Then why had she been frightened?

"Don't have anything else to do with Zack. Call the police if he comes within twenty yards of you." Wayne's directions were clear, concise and beyond negotiation.

Jessie tried to control the direction of her gaze, but she sensed Todd getting ready to speak. Although Jessie shot him a look of caution, it came too late.

"What?" Wayne looked from Jessie to Todd. "You *have* gotten out of your contract, haven't you?"

Dead silence greeted his question.

He demanded, "Haven't you?"

With a fluttering gesture, Todd spoke up. "Sheriff, hey, listen. I can explain. I've told Zack how she feels, and he's promised not to hassle her."

For the first time, Wayne addressed Todd. "What do you call his visit yesterday?"

"It's clear enough to me. He asked for a favor and she brushed him off. That's no reason to break a contract."

"Did you persuade her to perform at Zack's again?"

"I certainly did." Todd stood as tall as he could. Even then he only came to Wayne's collar. "Being on Zack's bad side would have been mucho disastrous. As her agent, I'm supposed to look after her career."

"The hell with her career."

Another silence descended.

Jessie eased out of the chair, distancing herself from Wayne. "But then," she said quietly, "it's not your career."

"Jessie's going to be a superstar," Todd said. "With the right handling."

Wayne turned on Todd. "Does that mean she has to be handled by people like Zack?"

Gesturing dismissively, Todd confided, "She's put the brakes on a dozen Zacks in her day. Jessie's not the sweet young thing she appears offstage, Sheriff. Besides, you call the shots in Claro County. You must have scared Zack spitless. She can run to you for as long as she's there."

"Todd, don't," Jessie said, moving in front of him. "Have I answered all your questions?" she asked Wayne.

"Have you heard anything I've said?" he came back at her.

"I think, perhaps, in this instance," she said, "I'll go along with my manager."

Muttering profanely, Wayne turned and left the room without a word of farewell.

FINISHING HER LAST SET, Jessie felt none of the customary exhilaration, only the emotional letdown and the physical fatigue.

She didn't bother to eat anything—her stomach was too jumpy—and after changing into street clothes, she asked the doorman to escort her to her car.

As they walked out the door, Wayne fell in step beside her.

Flashing his badge, he told the other man, "I'm Sheriff Jackson from Claro County. I'm here to see Ms. Reynolds home."

The doorman glanced at her questioningly.

She nodded. "It's all right, I know him."

"You didn't think you'd seen the last of me, did you?" he asked when they were alone.

"I wasn't sure what to think. As far as I'm concerned, you're totally unpredictable."

"I know. It scares the hell out of me." He opened her car door and inspected the interior. "I'm following you home," he announced. "We haven't finished our talk."

What scared the hell out of Jessie during the drive back to her apartment was the reaction she was having to the man. She turned into her driveway, as Wayne parked his truck at the curb in front of Mrs. Peters's sidewalk. The television was on in her living room, and Jessie saw the curtain twitch by Mrs. Peters's sofa which meant she was taking note of Jessie's company.

As Jessie climbed the stairs, Wayne caught up with her. He stood behind her while she unlocked her door. Following her inside, he offered no comment.

Unable to stand the silence any longer, she rushed into speech. "Would you like a beer? I don't think Patrick drank all of them."

"Patrick?"

Somehow the one word held a host of questions.

"My sound engineer. He supervises my recordings. He came over last night for supper."

"You're just surrounded by helpful males."

She stared at him, puzzled. "What's that supposed to mean?"

"Nothing," he muttered and changed the subject. "You realize Berkley is an idiot."

Poor Todd. Nobody liked him.

"He's not a bad agent. Just single-minded."

"He's using you."

"We use each other," she said. "That's the nature of the game. The better each of us does, the
better we both do."

"I don't think he has your best interests at heart."

"But then you and I don't agree on my best interests."

"How about safety? Your right to privacy?
Your—your integrity?"

"My *what?*"

"By agreeing to perform at Zack's you've as much
as given Zack permission to sexually harass you."

"That's not true."

"Isn't it?"

She shook her head restively. "I'll take my
chances."

"Not if I have anything to say about it."

"You don't," she said.

"The hell I don't!"

He grabbed her shoulders.

Her eyes widened. She wasn't sure whether she
should melt in his arms or push him way.

Making the decision for her, he swung away, cursing. After a few deep breaths he faced her again.

"How have you been?" he asked as if nothing had happened.

With her mouth gaping open, it was hard to answer. She licked her lips and tried to speak normally. "Fine, thank you. It's only been a week and a half." A week and a half that had seemed like an instant. And yet, a lifetime.

"How have *you* been?" She returned the query with irony.

After thinking for a moment, he smiled wryly. "You're right. It's a stupid question."

After a long silence, she asked abruptly, "Were you in the audience tonight for my first set?"

"Could you tell?"

"Yes. I almost couldn't finish. I—I thought...." She turned away from him, blushing. "Never mind what I thought."

Wayne began to prowl the room. "Greer tells me you saved his life."

"You talked to Lenny? Why?"

"Police business."

"Is that how you found out Zack had been here?"

"Did you save his life?"

"Not really. I was just there until the ambulance came."

Wayne took a book out of her bookcase. "Are you really going to appear at Zack's again?"

She started toward the kitchen. "That topic's off-limits. Are you on duty or would you like a beer? I also have tea or a soft drink."

"A soft drink will do. So—" his eyes followed her movements "—have you and Greer seen much of each other?"

That stopped her in her tracks. "Do you know you sound jealous?"

"I am—dammit." He tossed the book on the couch and started toward her.

She slipped by him and into the kitchen. Staring into the refrigerator, she tried to gather her thoughts.

After taking out two cans of soda, she turned. He was leaning against the cabinet, blocking her exit like a chunk of granite.

A living, breathing, sexy chunk of male granite.

"Are you in Austin on business?" she asked for something to say.

"That's what I told myself on the road into Austin this evening."

"And?"

"I lied."

"And I guess Zack's the reason you came by Kickers?"

"Yeah. I told myself that."

"And..."

"I lied."

"I'm glad."

"That I've been dishonest with myself."

"That you came by Kickers. It's good to see you if only for a while."

"Yeah." He moved closer. "It's good to see you, too."

She heard a ragged sigh and realized she had drawn it.

"How—how's crime in Crystal Creek?" she asked.

"Nothing I can't handle."

She laughed shakily. "You really are an arrogant man. You come stomping into my dressing room, ordering me around, treating Todd like an irritating insect." She grinned at a thought. "Warning Claudia off without a word. I have to admit, that was impressive."

His grin was lazy. "Claudia's not my type."

"I'm not, either. At least that's what you informed me."

"Never had a man walk away from you before, have you?"

He was cocky as well as arrogant.

"Have I yet? Remember, you lie. I'm beginning to wonder."

"I don't lie about some things." He moved closer still.

She put her hand on his chest as if to hold him off. Or maybe it was because she needed to touch him. "I hope you don't expect me to be sympathetic to your frustrated jealousy. You don't have the right to be possessive about something that's not yours."

"We've already agreed that my lack of possession isn't for want of invitation."

She managed a chuckle. "You're something else, Sheriff. Perhaps you'd better leave."

He shook his head slowly. "Not yet. Do you know what I wondered tonight when I watched you?"

"You damn near undressed me."

"I did more than damn near." He took a single finger and ran it down her cheek. "I wondered if your skin was as soft as it was translucent. I never really had the chance to find out for myself."

"Is it?" she whispered.

"I need more evidence." His hand skimmed her throat before it cupped the back of her neck.

"How much evidence do you need?"

He sighed hoarsely, urging her toward him. "An entire night's worth. But a kiss will have to do."

His mouth covered hers.

For a moment, they were still, absorbing the meeting. Then he began to leisurely outline her lips with his.

This kiss was different from the kiss in the truck.

That first kiss had been demanding. It had reeked of frustration and ambivalence.

This kiss was gentle and infinitely more seductive. This kiss waited for her to do the pleading. This kiss said they had all the time in the world.

It lied, Jessie knew. But she was past caring. Especially when he ran his tongue over her bottom lip asking for entrance. When she whimpered her eagerness, he plunged inside. At the same time he pressed her back against the counter until their bodies met and seduced and pleaded.

She flung her arms around his neck and held on tightly, needing his steadiness in the midst of her turbulent desire.

His hands began to skitter over the summer dress she wore. Bunching the fabric, finding its zipper, smoothing away the cotton so that he could splay his hand across her back. He followed her spine down to the slope of her waist. Cupping her side and slipping upward, his fingers brushed the swell of her breast.

She moaned and felt his hardness high against her.

"You know," she gasped, caution evaporating in the heat they generated, "this would work better if we were in bed."

The words filtered through to him and his whole body stiffened. "God—what are we doing?" he said, breaking away.

"I don't know," she answered helplessly. "You don't come with instructions." She took heaving breaths.

With great effort he staggered to the refrigerator and leaned his hands on it.

"Oh, God. I'm a fool to come near you."

His words were harsh sighs, stripping away her self-respect.

"Then go away," she cried, flinging out her arms defensively. "Do what you told *me* to do. Leave and stay away. I don't need some overgrown, overbearing cop messing up my life." She wiped away a tear she hadn't known was forming.

His gaze was somber as it settled over her face. "I'm sorry, Jessie," he said. "This is all my fault. I take full responsibility."

"It's nobody's fault," she came back wearily. "We both knew better. Look—neither one of us wants to get involved with the other."

He grunted a response.

"All we need to do is make the break final. I'll call Lenny if there's anything I need."

He muttered something vaguely affirmative.

"Since this is my house," she reminded him with as much dignity as she could muster, "I believe this time, it's your turn to leave."

Still not moving, he stared at her.

"Either go or stay," she burst out. "One or the other. But please let me off this roller coaster ride."

She pushed by him and ran to her bedroom, banging the door behind her. She couldn't bear to face him an instant longer.

Sounds of his departure filtered into the closed bedroom. She came out, peered around and turned the apartment door latch so she was locked safely inside.

Alone. There was hardly a trace of him left in her apartment. Only the unopened can of soda in the kitchen and the single book he'd tossed on the couch.

She went over and examined the title. It was a paperback she'd bought on Western folklore. She'd used some of its stories in composing her songs. Was he interested in folklore?

She knew so little about him. His tastes, his habits. There was barely a hint of who he was in her mind.

The only trace of him was on her body. She could still feel the pressure of his sex against her stomach. She reached around to the opened zipper down her back. The caressing air reminded her of the heat in his fingers. Her lips were still swollen from his gentle ravaging. The moisture between her legs was evidence of how much she'd wanted him. The flush lingering beneath her skin was the residue of the desire he'd evoked.

With a groan, she grabbed one of the soft drink cans and chugalugged it, needing something—anything—to wash away the taste of him in her mouth. Having begun with a soda, she peered into the cabinet. She realized she hadn't eaten since lunch.

Perhaps she'd heat a cup of soup like the one she'd asked for earlier. She put a cup of water in the microwave, set the timer and stared at the revolving turntable stupidly.

Rousing herself after a moment, she went to the bedroom to strip down and throw on a robe. By then, the timer had rung and the water was steaming.

She emptied a packet of soup mix into the cup and began to stir. That was about all she was capable of doing, she realized. Stirring noodle soup and remembering.

When she heard the knock on the door, she groaned. It could be Mrs. Peters checking to see if she was all right after the strange man's visit. It could even be Todd.

Please, don't let it be Todd and Claudia. Jessie didn't think she could speak civilly to them.

Tying her robe more securely around her, she went to face the worst.

Wayne stood outside in the shadows of the night. Without giving her a chance to refuse him, he came in, shut and locked the door behind him.

"Wha—?"

"I'm staying."

"Wha—?"

"Don't say a word."

His hand covered her lips for a moment before his mouth claimed her. The kiss this time had the feel of possession. If she'd wanted to protest, he was giving her no chance.

She didn't want to. Oh, how she didn't want to.

Instead, she let herself collapse against him. She needed him to hold her. And hold her and hold her. And make love to her again and again through the night.

"You don't have anything on under the robe, do you?" he asked, exploring its texture.

"No."

"How convenient." His tone was light, but she could hear the strain underneath.

He pulled away from her just long enough to untie the belt and slip his hands inside to slide along her skin. She felt his faint trembling.

She shivered with his touch and couldn't help saying, "You're not going to turn around and leave, are you?"

"No. Not again. I've spent the longest twenty minutes of my life, driving around Austin like a madman. I ached so bad, I almost had a wreck."

He took one of her hands and rubbed it against his erection. Even as he did, he groaned and pulled her hand away.

"Too much. Not yet," he muttered into her earlobe. Running his hands down and over her rear, he rubbed her stomach against him.

"Tell me now. Do you want me to leave?" He asked the question even as he was awakening longings.

"No. I've spent the past twenty minutes unable to do a thing."

"You managed to do one constructive thing," he said, shifting his hands up her ribs.

As his fingers brushed her breasts, she shivered with pleasure.

But there was one last thing she had to say. "Are you sure this is right?"

His eyes closed momentarily. "I know it's inevitable."

"But what about tomorrow?"

"We'll worry about it then."

"Wayne—" She pulled away to look at him.

He stared down at her, the easiness deserting his expression. His body tensed as though he still was struggling with his ambivalence. A bleak look flickered and then was blotted out by desire.

"I can't keep away from you," he finally confessed. "That's the goddamned truth of it. And now that I'm holding you, I can't let go. The only way I'll walk out of this apartment tonight is if you send me away. Are you going to?"

"I can't," she whispered. "I can't stop wanting you. When I saw you tonight, I thought my heart would burst with desire."

He gathered her to him. "My God, how could any one woman feel so good?"

She reached around his neck and stood on her tiptoes.

"You know," he said, swinging her up into his arms, "this would work better if we were in bed."

CHAPTER EIGHT

JESSIE TIGHTENED her arms around him. "That's my line, isn't it?"

"When I left you—" his breath fanned her brow "—I kept remembering the way you'd said it. As if you couldn't hang on to the words."

"Right now," she breathed, "the only thing I can hang on to is you."

He chuckled huskily, but she could still sense him holding on to his control.

Making his way to her bedroom, he found the bedside lamp casting a glow against the walls and ceiling. When he laid her against the spread, the play of light and shadow etched a landscape along her curves.

The pure white of her robe framed her like a painting. Drawing it away from her, he stood motionless, intent on his visual pleasure.

She flushed with desire as his eyes lingered over her.

"I've wanted to see you like this from the moment I first glimpsed you," he said. "I've never been obsessed with a woman's body before. I thought I was immune to physical beauty."

"I have the usual equipment." She was shaken by his tone. "It functions in all the normal ways."

He ran a single finger along her rosy cheek. "It's how it all fits together that fascinates me. It's how it heats for me."

"I'm glad you like it," she whispered.

He smiled faintly and allowed his hand to settle like a feather over one breast.

It was the only place he touched her. Somehow that made the contact all the more intimate. Without being conscious of it, she stirred on the bed.

She reached to unbutton his shirt, and her hands claimed territory in the tangle on his chest. Her fingernails made faint furrows along his warm skin.

He shuddered. She could feel his muscles tightening, his control cracking. Still, he held his body in check. Only his gaze scorched her, making her melt inside.

She'd never had a man's eyes make love to her before. She found it wildly exciting. She heard herself whimpering. Her expression grew pleading.

"What?" he asked.

She arched her back provocatively.

"Is this what you want?" His fingers plucked at her nipple.

The whimper inside her throat turned into a growl. "I want more than that." Seeking out the nubs hidden in his fur, she brushed her thumbs over them. His shudder this time ended in a sigh.

"It's not fair," she went on. "My view's not nearly so interesting."

"You mean this?" He shrugged off his shirt.

"Can I help you with your jeans?"

He grinned lopsidedly. "I'd better not risk it."

When he pulled down his jeans and shorts, his sex spilled out, engorged and thrusting. Soon he was naked, his shadow enormous on the wall.

"You're quite a handful." Her look roamed up and down him.

When his brow arched quizzically, she realized how he'd taken her statement. "I meant all of you." She knew he was enjoying her embarrassment. "Come here," she instructed him. "You're too far away."

"Is this close enough?" he said, sinking to his knees on the mattress.

When she held out her hand, he was still out of reach.

"No," she muttered.

"How about this?" He leaned over her, a palm on either side of her shoulders.

"That's more like it." She ran her nails along his ribs.

He gave another involuntary shiver, but still he didn't lower himself against her. She was growing frantic for the contact. She put her arms around his back, tugging him down.

"What's keeping you?" she asked, edgy with passion.

"I'm not sure I can touch you. I've waited too long for this." He closed his eyes for a moment as longing washed over his features. "Once I begin, it won't last."

"I want it quick. I want you." She cradled his erection. "Come to me," she whispered, urged on by her desire.

"Aaaaah..." he gasped, pushing hard into her palm as she continued to fondle him.

And finally, she got what she wanted. Something inside him snapped, his restraint fractured. His flesh pressed against hers, hot and possessive. His mouth covered hers in a frenzied kiss.

Gone was the restrained lover. She'd let loose a primitive creature. A creature who commanded a shameless response.

His hands claimed her flesh. His tongue thrust inside her. He slid his fingers between her legs and searched out her heat.

"You're ready," he said fiercely, stroking her, goading her.

Spreading her thighs, she moaned, "Don't wait."

"I can't," he said and knelt before her, taking only enough time to unwrap a foil package.

Positioning her legs wide, raising her hips high to meet him until she lay open and wanton, he clamped his hands around her waist. "This time it's quick."

He plunged inside her. His grasp directed her body as she sheathed and unsheathed him. He lunged deeper, deeper.

Her senses whirled at his demands.

"This time...this time..." she panted, the rhythm overtaking her. Her hands climbed his legs and clutched at his sides. The need...the need...driving her...driving her...

"Come for me," he ordered.

His thumbs searched out her sex and began to torture her with pleasure.

"I...I—" But words weren't enough.

She sobbed out her release and pulsed all around him. He spilled deep inside her, crying out her name.

IT WAS A LONG five minutes before either of them could speak.

"I came," she said, her thoughts so confused she forgot to censor them.

"I noticed." He rolled on his back so that she was draped over his chest. He took the opportunity to let his fingers wander along the slope of her spine.

"I mean—you told me to and I did. Just like that." Her breath caught jerkily. She was dazed by the experience.

He chuckled. "I hope you're always this cooperative."

"No. No—you don't understand." She remembered the years when sex had become a lesson in loneliness. When more and more, she'd felt less and less.

She raised herself on her hands, her expression bewildered. "You bring something out in me. It's never been like this before."

His fingers slipped through her hair, luxuriating in its texture until his hands framed her face so that she had to meet his gaze.

"It was there waiting for me." He kissed her gently. "Didn't you feel it?"

"I—I didn't know."

"The way you blaze onstage, I knew you could blaze in my arms. I was right."

But that was just it. No man had ever ignited her. The passion she'd experienced, she'd poured into her songs. Now she felt sated, her restlessness deserting her. She was content to shelter in this man's arms.

The thought disturbed her peace. She tried to pull away from him.

"What's the matter?" he asked, holding her close.

"Nothing," she lied.

He turned her over so that she was a captive beneath him.

"You surprised yourself," he said. "That's no reason to be frightened."

Yes. But she wasn't ready for their lovemaking to be such an earth-shaking event.

She searched his features to find the male creature she'd writhed with on the bed. "You surprised me, too. You—you're usually so controlled."

His smile was wry. "I warned you what would happen when I finally got hold of you. I've had a hard-on for the past week and a half."

Her lashes fluttered shut. "From what I can tell, you're not far from one now."

He rubbed himself against her. "You're amazingly perceptive."

His lazy sensuality scattered her disturbed thoughts. Besides, he'd told her they would worry later.

"You aim to do anything about it anytime soon?" she asked with a lift of her eyebrows.

"I expect so," he drawled. "Any minute now." He propped himself on his elbow. "I have a couple of things I aim to do first."

"Can I help?" She started to reach up for him.

"No. Lie back." His hand was gentle but firm as it covered her shoulder. "The first time took the edge off. Now I mean to savor you." His mouth covered hers in a slow hungry kiss.

His voice was husky when he pulled away to say, "I'm greedy for you. I want to smell you, to taste you, to touch you, to know you. So that when my hand finds you in the dark—" he splayed his palm over her stomach "—I'll never lose my place."

"Aaahh," she breathed out. His words and kiss had already aroused her. The ache between her legs had started to heat. Since she wasn't sure of his intentions, she could only lie quiescent. This time, without doubt, he was calling the shots.

"For instance—" he buried his nose in her hair and breathed in the scent of her "—you smell good all over. Essence of woman." His hand wandered up her leg and loitered over her rib cage. "Your skin's like warm satin everywhere I touch."

His face slid down her throat and across one breast. His mouth opened over it and he suckled at her nipple.

She murmured her delight, too languorous to move.

"You taste like dark silken nights," he whispered, wetting her other breast. "Your flesh is sweet and tender." His teeth nibbled delicately.

"Y-you're doing things to me." She could barely get out the words.

"What?" he asked. His mouth sought her navel before trailing down her stomach. "Where...? Where am I doing things? Here? Here...?"

"Yes. Oh, yes," she cried out her pleasure.

"You taste like spice," he murmured, his tongue laving the nub of her sex.

"Wayne...Wayne—" Her need was beginning to consume her just as his mouth was.

"What do you want?"

"I—"

"Come to me," he crooned. "Come to me, Jessie—" His finger delved inside her as insistent as his mouth.

With a sob and a moan she came...over and over...until she was dazed with sensations.

Only then did he move over her and fit himself inside her, plunging, plunging, more and more urgently. "Come to me again." His voice was guttural with desire. "I want to feel you throb around me."

To her dazzled astonishment she did as he asked.

WHEN JESSIE AWAKENED the dark was fading into dawn. The clock by her bed read six-thirty. She'd slept three hours in the circle of Wayne's body.

One of his rangy legs rested amid hers, the other hung over the end of the bed frame. He lay on his side, his biceps pillowing her neck, a muscular forearm slung over her midriff. If she turned her head, her lips could taste the male scent on his broad, solid chest.

She felt diminutive next to his bulk. It was as though she'd discovered a giant tangled in her bed sheets. She remembered vaguely when he'd pulled them down and coaxed her between them. When he'd gathered her up, and she'd nestled in to him as if he were a haven she'd found.

She remembered other things, including his truck parked beside the curb.

Mrs. Peters was sure to be curious when she saw it and realized that the strange man who'd left had come back to spend the night. No one had before, Jessie realized. In fact, she hadn't slept with a man since she'd moved here. That admission caught her up short.

Had her celibacy made her vulnerable to Wayne? Their lovemaking was unique in her sexual experience. She'd never slept with a man before who'd totally possessed her. Who'd wrested so much from her. She wasn't sure at this moment if she were even whole.

More disturbing, she wasn't sure where she stopped and he began. Sometime during their coupling, their passion, like a torch, had welded them together.

Lying still and cautious, Jessie knew that ordinarily she would have dozed another few hours. But she desperately needed to be separate and away from the man on the bed beside her.

Sliding gingerly from under his loose embrace, Jessie scooped her robe off the floor where Wayne had tossed it.

He must have sensed her leaving because he grumbled in his sleep, then cradled her pillow and was peacefully quiet.

She tiptoed across the room and shut the door as she left.

On her way to the bathroom, she shrugged the robe over her nakedness. But she couldn't hide her face when it stared back at her from the lavatory mirror.

She looked stunned. That was the only word for it. Her hair was a tangled mess, her lips were swollen. Without makeup her complexion was as pale as a pearl.

Her eyes were wide with new bewildering knowledge. She could see the pulse in her neck jump. And she wasn't sure whether the agitation came from ecstasy or fear.

Her soul felt just as naked as her pale features. Somehow she had to climb back into herself and find armor to protect her. What she needed was a cup of coffee to lend her energy if not strength.

Taking her hairbrush along to begin its tortuous chore, she padded into the kitchen and set up the coffeepot. Automatically she glanced into the refrigerator, looking for a breakfast she could serve her overnight guest. After all, her mom had taught her to always be hospitable.

As if she hadn't been already! Jessie smothered her giggle at the absurd thought.

Brushing her tangles methodically she waited for the coffee. When it had finished dripping, she poured a cup and went into the living room. She sat Indian fashion on the floor, leaning her back against the couch.

Now—maybe she could think. Alone like this, she hoped she could regain perspective. And perhaps make sense out of what had occurred.

What had happened exactly? In twenty-five words or less.

Wayne had wanted her. She'd wanted him. He'd taken her, she'd let him. And he would wake up any minute and go his own way.

She counted her words with a perverse amusement. Right on the money. How could such a few simple words cover the complexity of events?

Was that really what he'd do when he woke up? Leave her without a forwarding address? She hadn't a clue.

So okay—she couldn't predict his mood or his actions. It was just as important to decide how she viewed the hours she'd just spent.

What did she plan to do about the episode?

Episode. An odd word to use, but it would have to serve. How did she want to remember it? How important was it to her? What part would it play in the days ahead?

This was how she tackled life—with planning and forethought. Taking events as they occurred and weaving them into a future of her own design.

There was only one catch. Not true, she thought. There were at least a million catches. The first being that she didn't know her mind any better than she did his. The images of their lovemaking snatched at her reason.

Her feelings were more hopelessly tangled than her hair. And there was nothing equivalent to her hairbrush to unravel them.

Unravel. She was coming unraveled. Sitting here alone wasn't solving a thing. If anything, thinking about Wayne had intensified her confusion.

It struck her forcefully that this wasn't a task she could perform by herself. All this sorting out and examining of choices. Her decisions would be molded by his decisions. Her emotions were inextricably entangled with his.

It was scary to realize she needed him this way. She'd left his side to reclaim her autonomy. Instead, she'd wound up feeling more enmeshed than before.

There must be something she held within herself. Something that was hers alone. Something his presence in her bed didn't change or complicate.

She glanced around the room before spotting the guitar.

Her panic subsided. Of course. Her music.

By losing herself in composing she could finally shut him out. Her music would be the armor that cloaked her vulnerability.

How heavily did he sleep? As sheriff, he probably woke up early most days. She'd have to take a chance that he was tired enough to remain oblivious another couple of hours. Because suddenly it was imperative that she sing and compose.

She found her mute and fastened it over the strings. If she strummed softly, the notes wouldn't filter into the bedroom. She'd work on the song that still lay buried in her soul.

"I hadn't planned on your coming . . . I thought I could choose . . . Who I let in my life . . . who I gave myself to . . ."

Her voice died away. Her fingers halted their slide along the strings. Her palm stilled the haunting echo.

This song couldn't be about him. She couldn't let it. If she did, the song would be his, and every time she sang it, he'd be in the room, within her.

She'd tinker with it some other time when the memories of last night had faded. When she had more options.

Taking a couple of deep breaths and willing her fingers to stop trembling, she began to work on a rip-roaring ditty about cowboys and cowgals and riding a horse until it knew who was master.

These lyrics and the melody came more easily, but every time her neurons began to hum with inspiration, she'd remember who was sprawled in the next room. Her mind would take off and she'd have to patiently corral it.

Dammit! She was not going to let that man complicate her entire life. It was as if "that man" had willed her to think of him, because the minute the phrase flashed through her head, she knew he was watching.

She looked up and found him lounging in the entrance to her bedroom. He had on his jeans, half buttoned up.

Now she remembered why she hadn't stopped to examine him when she'd left earlier. She only had to study him for her heart to founder.

"Why did you get up?" he asked. "I wasn't finished snuggling."

She shrugged. "I was restless."

"Is this what you do when you get restless? Write another song?"

"I guess."

"I have a better suggestion." He roused himself from the doorframe and started to advance upon her.

Instinctively, she jumped onto the couch, clutching her guitar in front of her as if to hold him at bay.

His look flared for a moment, then smoothed out enigmatically. "You once told me you used your music as an escape."

"That's not exactly how I put it."

He brushed aside her protest. "Is that what you're trying to do, retreat from me and what happened? Or are you just trying to run away from yourself?"

"I don't know what you mean."

Shaking his head sorrowfully, he came dangerously closer. "Now you're the one who's lying."

"I don't—"

"Why don't you admit that the way we made love shook the hell out of you?"

In a crouched position, Jessie found it hard to inch backward. Instead, descending from the couch with as much dignity as she could muster, she put her instrument on top of the bookcase and tried to circle around him, heading in the direction of the bathroom.

She should have known he wouldn't let her get away so easily.

Catching hold of her wrist, he swung her around so they were face-to-face.

"Where are you going?" he asked, as if it didn't really matter.

She found it impossible to reply.

He leaned over so that his breath warmed her neck. "Haven't you found out, you can't run from some things?"

"I'm not trying to run," she sputtered. "I'm just trying to find myself again." She closed her eyes, appalled at what she'd just admitted.

His hands moved to her waist. "Don't you think you were yourself," he murmured, "when you begged me to take you? Or should I say 'ordered'?"

She choked out a denial.

"Do you think you were someone else when you moaned in my arms?"

She flung her hands over her ears. He had to duck to miss getting slapped by her flailing. When she tried to twist away, he picked her up without noticeable effort and headed for the bedroom.

"I thought you said you didn't use your size to get your way," she said peevishly.

"That's not exactly how I put it."

"Well, that's what you're doing. Slinging me around like a sack of potatoes."

"You mean like this?" He tumbled her onto the bed. "Don't think you can get rid of me—just by picking up your guitar."

"I don't know what to think. That's the problem. I hate depending on someone else to know my own mind."

"I see. So that's what's bothering you. You can't categorize what's happened between us."

"I don't even know what I want to happen next."

"I have a few ideas for the immediate future." He nibbled down the side of her throat.

"But that will just put me where I was before."

"That's where I want you."

"But I can't think."

"You're not supposed to."

"But I don't know who I am," she wailed.

"Right at this moment you're mine."

His tongue outlined her ear and dipped into it, making her shiver with helpless delight. He nibbled his way to her mouth and conducted lightning forays inside, making her yearn for a deeper possession.

His hand worried a nipple, and need coursed through her. One of his thighs insinuated itself between hers.

He was teasing her. Tempting her. Seducing her.

And he was succeeding. She could no more withstand his erotic assault than she could stop breathing. When his mouth traveled to her breasts, ravishing them equally, she grabbed hold of him wildly and buried her face in his hair.

As he teased and tormented her, he stayed in total control. It wasn't like the first time they'd made love, when he'd lost any semblance of restraint or consciousness. Nor was it like the second time when she'd felt like a six-course dinner.

This time—this time—she knew he was making a point. And she couldn't stop him. She didn't want to.

But somewhere beyond the necessity of passion it galled her that he could drag her back at will from wherever she'd been.

He was relentless, determined. Her body responded tumultuously. He brought her to climax until she was faint. Then he moved into her and brought them both to orgasm.

Afterward, exhausted, she fell into sleep.

THE NEXT TIME Jessie surfaced, Wayne was the one who'd left the bedroom. Looking around she realized his clothes had vanished. For an instant she panicked. Had he left without saying goodbye?

Then, through the open door she smelled the scents of breakfast. Instead of cooking for her guest, her guest was cooking for her.

As Jessie swung her feet off the bed she noted soreness in some interesting muscles. She groaned her discomfort and headed for the bathroom, grabbing some clothes along the way.

This time when she faced Wayne, she wanted to be poised and collected. It was hard to be in control, naked as a jaybird. She'd already found that out.

A shower would help as well. The drenching spray would wash away his handprints. As long as she didn't expect a little soap and water to wash away his handiwork. She had a feeling she was marked for life.

Ten minutes later she walked out of the bathroom, damp but demure and feeling considerably less vulnerable. Her hair was caught back in a low ponytail. The shirt she'd selected swallowed up her torso. And her loose trousers obscured the line of her hips.

None of this preparation, however, provided her with conversation. She could only stare dumbly as he deftly flipped an omelet.

Glancing her way, he smiled, then went on with his task.

"I'm supposed to be doing that," she said. "You're my guest."

When he looked at her quizzically, she turned bright red.

"Actually—" she cleared her throat "—I haven't had much practice with overnight guests. I hope Mrs. Peters hasn't had a coronary."

"Mrs. Peters?"

"My landlady."

"Why should she?"

"Your truck's been parked in front of her house on and off since two-thirty this morning. I'm sure she's noticed. She feels the need to look after me."

"Oh. I see."

He didn't continue, and the silence suggested they'd exhausted that subject. She searched for another.

"Sit down," he instructed her, rescuing her from her dilemma. She looked around and realized he'd set the stamp-sized table with orange juice and coffee. After she settled, he put a third of the omelet in front of her, along with a helping of grits. Both portions were generous.

"Cream? Sugar?" He might have been the host.

"No, thank you," she said politely. "I drink my coffee black."

For a while the silence between them was interrupted by the clinking of silverware and china. But it didn't take long for them to empty their plates. Jessie noted that the omelet was delicious. And that Wayne's appetite was proportionate to his stature.

And if the wet towels in the bathroom hadn't already alerted her, she would have guessed from his springy hair that he'd taken a shower while she slept.

No man should look that sexy in crumpled clothes, she decided. No man should look that sexy and be able to cook.

After refilling his coffee cup, Wayne settled back in his chair. His legs were too long for the table and he slanted them to the side of it. His gaze was steady as it met hers head on.

"Come up next weekend and stay with me," he said.

Her jaw dropped open.

"Well?" he prompted after a gaping moment.

As though she had an answer!

"I can't," she said. "My days off are Sunday and Monday."

"Come Sunday then. I'll switch schedules with Bobby. He needs to keep his pants on. Best way for him to do that is to stay on duty while LouAnn's free."

Jessie decided she must be in a dream. Who were Bobby and LouAnn? And why were Wayne and she having this extraordinary conversation?

She shook her head to clear it. "Have I missed something along the way?"

"I don't think so," he said reasonably.

"But—"

"What do you want to do, Jessie? Talk this thing to death? It wouldn't work, even if we tried it."

"But—"

"Besides, I don't really think there's anything to say."

"But—?"

"Did you expect this to be a one-night stand?"

She shook her head frantically.

"Well, then—I'll see you next Sunday at my place or yours. Better make it mine. I coach Little League on Monday."

His verbal maneuvering took her breath away.

After a couple of gusty sighs she managed to ask, "Won't Crystal Creek be surprised that its upstanding sheriff has a female house guest?"

He grinned. "They'd be more surprised if it were a male."

She rolled her eyes at his attempt at humor.

"Besides, it's all over town," he said, "that I kissed you in the First Baptist parking lot."

"Yes, I know," she murmured.

"I figure the whole town will be disappointed if nothing comes of that. Come on—" he rose from his chair and started toward the door, sweeping her up beside him "—I called in to the office to say I'd be late. But if I don't make it back soon, Alberta will skin me."

Just before he stepped out on the porch, he turned and framed her face. For a moment she saw behind the matter-of-fact facade to his brooding intensity.

But the kiss he gave her was infinitely gentle. His voice when he spoke was as hushed and tender as a spring breeze.

"Jessie—we can't stop seeing each other. You realize that, don't you?"

She nodded.

"That means—"

He paused, leaving her more troubled than before. He must have seen the depth of her anxiety because before he began again, he kissed her eyes shut with care and deliberation.

She had the strange notion that he was unwilling for her to see the pain in his.

"That means—" he repeated the words even more tenderly "—that we have to find our way from here."

CHAPTER NINE

IT HAD BEEN A WHILE since Wayne had looked down the barrel of a gun. He thought he'd wised up enough to avoid tight situations. Yet here he was on a hazy summer day standing beside his patrol car trying to talk a kid into handing over a semiautomatic. All the time the grass along the side of the road rustled with the wind and the cicadas chirped in the waves of heat. It wasn't why or where Wayne would have chosen to meet his maker.

"Now, son," he said with deliberation. "You don't want to go and point a gun at a law officer."

The boy couldn't have been eighteen. His hands shook visibly as he raised the weapon higher. "Don't come any closer," he warned in a quivering voice. "I—I'm not afraid t-to use this."

Wayne lifted his hands. "I'm not coming closer. But I want you to think about putting the gun down."

"I can't. You'll arrest me." The boy glanced toward his car.

Wayne guessed the car was either hot or loaded with drugs like the boy.

"I'm gonna leave," the boy said, his finger twitching over the hair trigger. "Don't try to follow me." He shifted his feet in the gravel.

Wayne stood absolutely still. One wrong twitch of that trembling finger and he'd have a bullet in his chest.

He weighed the options available to him.

The kid hadn't thought to tell Wayne to unholster his weapon. He was so confused he didn't remember that other cars would come by.

All that bothered the boy was that Wayne had stopped him. "Why did you pull in front of me?" A sob tore out of his throat. "You're gonna make me shoot you."

Wayne swallowed the cotton in his mouth, knowing it was a wonder the gun hadn't already discharged.

"Your left rear tire looked flat," he said. "I thought you'd want to know."

"My tire?" The boy was dazed enough to be taken in by Wayne's ploy. He bent to inspect the wheel.

Wayne didn't miss the opportunity. In a flash he kicked away the gun, which fired harmlessly into the ground.

The boy's arms were behind his back before he knew what was happening. Since he couldn't have topped the scales at more than a hundred and thirty pounds, Wayne hadn't had much difficulty.

After taking a moment to appreciate the fact he was alive, Wayne secured the youth with a pair of handcuffs and led him to the black-and-white.

As Wayne started his engine, the radio came alive with Alberta's strained voice. A motorist, she informed him, had just called in to the office on his car phone with a wild story about a deputy being held up by the side of the road.

The story was true, Wayne told her. But the incident was over, he was safe, and the perpetrator was in custody.

By the time Wayne drove into Crystal Creek, the boy, whose name was Mike, had broken into wrenching sobs. If Wayne was any judge, Mike was coming off crack with a vengeance. He was probably no more than sixteen years old.

A short time later, Wayne guided the youth into the holding tank of the county jail. He sat him down gently and patted the boy's shoulder with a calming hand. "We're going to get you some help, Mike," he said.

"Alberta," he called, "would you phone Dr. Purdy and see if you can bring him a prisoner to check over right away? Tell him he's pretty hopped up. Almost ran off the Route Forty bridge."

In a moment Alberta announced, "Dr. Purdy says bring him right over to the clinic. You ready for me to take him?"

"In a minute." Wayne unloaded Mike's gun carefully and placed the clip and weapon in the safe.

Alberta's brows flew up. "So that's what he was carrying."

"When they find out what I've done, they'll kill me," Mike cried.

Alberta's gaze met Wayne's. Her sober expression said more than words could.

"Nobody's going to kill anybody," Wayne said to Mike. He sat across from the boy so that they were face-to-face. "You want to tell us who 'they' are and where you live?"

Putting his head in his hands, Mike shook his head despairingly.

"Bobby—?" Wayne beckoned his deputy. "Work on finding Mike's address so you can contact his family."

"You got his driver's license?" Bobby asked as he came into the tank.

"He wasn't carrying one. Have Pete tow in a red Camaro on Route Forty near the bridge." He tossed Bobby a set of keys.

"Here's the license number." He handed Bobby a strip of paper. "Check its registration. You should be able to get an address from that."

"You think the Camaro's hot?"

Wayne shook his head. "When Alberta checked the computer, it hadn't been reported. Besides, look at the key ring. It's personalized. I want his family here on the double. Without parental consent, Doc Purdy can only provide emergency treatment."

"You sure he has folks?" Bobby asked.

Studying Mike for a moment, Wayne nodded. "I'm sure."

He went on with his instructions. "The Camaro probably has drugs stowed away in it. I think that's why he panicked and drew the gun. I'm going to get a search warrant, although we have ample cause without one. But I don't want his parents to have any gripes about the way we've handled this case. I have a feeling—"

Bobby nodded knowingly.

They'd both seen kids who'd been given too much money to make up for not enough attention. Their parents were usually the ones who were the most aggressive. And the least likely to want to hear what an officer had to say.

Wayne suspected they'd have plenty to talk about. If he was right, Mike had been dealing drugs from his car.

After Alberta left with Mike, and Bobby got busy tracking down the family, Wayne went into his office and sank into his chair.

He didn't, however, call the county judge to ask for a warrant. He'd get to that in a minute.

Instead, staring out the barred windows onto the courthouse lawn, he sipped a cup of coffee to calm his jumping nerves, wished he had one of the cigarettes he'd given up three years ago, and berated himself soundly.

He could have gotten himself killed, and a sixteen-year-old kid convicted for capital murder. All because he'd lost that edge of concentration. Because he'd been thinking of Jessie and Tuesday night.

Something had to change. Somehow he had to figure out how to contain this relationship. Yet how was he ever going to fit her into a corner in his life?

Hell, it had barely been forty-eight hours, and he was impatient to phone her. He wanted to hear her voice so he'd know she was real.

"Wayne?" Bobby knocked on the door.

"Come in," Wayne instructed.

"The Camaro's registered to a Michael Skinner, Sr., in Fredericksburg. In Gillespie County. How far is Fredericksburg? About forty miles?"

Wayne nodded.

"Well, I called up the Gillespie County Sheriff's Office to see if they knew anything about a kid named Mike who drove a Camaro. They knew plenty. They also suspect he's been doing drugs."

"Sit down," Wayne said, using his boot to direct a chair in Bobby's direction. "And tell me everything you heard."

Wayne wasn't surprised when he found out the Skinners owned several businesses in Fredericksburg. A Camaro was an expensive toy for a teenager. Nor was he surprised when he learned that Michael, Jr., had run in and out of trouble with the law. His parents' usual response to the scrapes had been "boys will be boys."

Well, that wouldn't cut it this time. Threatening an officer with a gun was a first-degree felony. Mike could be sent to a correctional facility until he was eighteen, then tried as an adult and carted off to prison.

Wayne and Bobby discussed notifying the parents and decided they'd ask the Gillespie County Sheriff's Office to do it. As Wayne expected, he received a phone call from an irate Mr. Skinner within thirty minutes.

Wayne figured it would be a long afternoon.

Five hours later, his prediction had proved accurate. Those hours had included tears, threats and a large dose of plain speaking by Wayne and Dr. Purdy.

By the end of their visit, Mr. and Mrs. Skinner were considerably shaken. Mike had been returned to their custody but only for as long as it took to check him into a drug treatment facility. And a Claro County judge would be overseeing the stay.

Sitting alone in his office as the dusk deepened, Wayne realized he hated cases like Mike's. So much promise. So much of it wasted. He wasn't sure whether the kid would make it or not.

Alberta had left. Bobby was off duty, Gilbert on patrol. Wayne knew he should stir himself and go grab a sandwich. For Nora's sake he still ate at the Longhorn Coffee Shop, but it was difficult for him, remembering Dottie.

He heard a noise in the outer office. When he opened his door he found Eugene with his hand poised to announce his arrival.

"Well, hello," Wayne said, not bothering to hide his surprise. "Fancy meeting you here."

Eugene waved a greeting as Wayne ushered him inside.

After offering a chair, Wayne leaned back in his and asked, "To what do I owe this honor? You said it would take an earthquake to get you back into this office."

"What the hell happened this afternoon?" Eugene asked, without preamble. "And—more important—how hard have you been on yourself about it?"

Trust Eugene to come to the point.

Wayne grinned shortly. "You're the first person to ask that question."

Eugene grunted. "That's because I'm pretty sure I know the answer."

Wayne's gaze met that of the older man. "I almost let a frightened kid put a bullet through me today, Eugene."

"That's what I heard. It's not like you to let your guard down." Eugene eyed his protégé thoughtfully. "You've got the quickest damn reflexes I ever saw. Remember the time you disarmed the son of a bitch who reached into his coat to pull out a Magnum."

"Today I wasn't facing an SOB. Just a hopped-up kid." Wayne paused, then went on gruffly. "I knew when I stopped him that he was high on something. He'd been weaving down the road like a rattler."

"So what's going on? I'm worried about you, son. Zack's been saying all over town that you've got it in for him."

"Has he?" Wayne shrugged. "I guess that comes with the territory."

"He claims it's because of Jessica Reynolds."

"She has nothing—" Wayne thought better of what he was about to say and changed it slightly. "She's not involved with this. You know why I'm investigating Zack."

"Crystal Creek thinks Zack may be right about your feuding. Although they would like a few more facts to go on."

"What do they have now?" Wayne asked, dreading the answer.

"The kiss, of course. There's also a lot of speculation about the night you spent in Austin. You have Alberta to thank for that."

"My God," Wayne muttered, "does everybody know everything about everyone in this town?"

"They sure do," Eugene said cheerfully. "I thought you'd lived here long enough to find that out."

"I guess I just haven't been in the rumor mill before."

"Don't you believe it. People have been pondering your marital status for years. How you're always so careful not to let a girl get her hopes up. How you're kind of detached about the whole damn thing."

Wayne grimaced. "Not a pleasant picture, is it?"

All you're looking for is a maid and baby factory...

"I don't make the gossip," Eugene said. "I just report it. People have also been wondering why you haven't taken up with the widow Cramer. But now that Ms. Reynolds is in the picture, people understand why you passed Denise over."

Leaning back in his chair, Wayne took on Eugene's direct gaze. "Why haven't you bothered to tell me this before?"

"I never worried about you before. You were never in danger of getting your head shot off. I expect Jessica Reynolds is quite a distraction."

Wayne pointed his finger angrily. "Don't blame her for this."

"I wouldn't think of it," Eugene said. "You're the one who's responsible for keeping your dick in your pants and out of your work."

"Is that what you came to tell me?" Wayne asked, his lips twitching.

"Part of it," Eugene said. He faced Wayne squarely. "I also came to tell you not to beat yourself up for making a mistake. I had my share. This won't be your last one."

There was a long moment of silence while the two men studied each other.

Finally Wayne blurted out, "Dammit, Eugene. It wasn't just me. That frightened kid could have gone to jail for life. Hell, he could have gotten the death penalty for shooting an officer."

"Well, he didn't. So cut yourself some slack."

Another long moment of silence ended with Wayne's wry grin. "Is that all you came to say?" he asked.

"For the moment," Eugene answered gruffly.

"Okay. I hear you. The point's well taken."

Eugene nodded his satisfaction. The subject was closed.

"Now answer a question of mine," Wayne said, crossing his arms over his chest. "Why should people care about who I go to bed with?"

"Because sex is basic. Like being born's basic. Crystal Creek has its priorities straight. New life coming in, carrying hopes and dreams into the future. Like J. T. McKinney's bride presenting him with a baby."

"What does that—"

"Who's sleeping with who," Eugene went on relentlessly, "that's serious business, too. It's not just climbing between the sheets. It's choosing who to spend a life with."

"Not necessarily."

"Ultimately it is. If lust is strong enough, it ends up in love or hate. Making love's not some trivial diversion from traffic jams and conference calls and skyscrapers and self-actualization and all that other crap. It's basic, son. As basic as death."

Wayne managed a smile. "I had no idea you had such strong feelings about modern life."

"I'm just grateful I never had to drive home from work on a freeway. One of the reasons you came here is because you felt the same. Crystal Creek's helped you let go of your past. Don't blame us for being curious about your future."

When Eugene put it like that, Wayne had no response.

Gilbert's entrance made a response unnecessary. To say that he was startled at seeing Eugene would be putting it mildly.

"Why, hello, Sheriff Nelson," he managed. "Good to see you."

"I was just leaving." Eugene did so without pause.

After his exit, Gilbert sagged against the desk. "I thought everybody had gone home. That the place was locked up. I heard the voices and didn't know what was going down. Man—you and Nelson might have ended up with a gun covering you."

"Wouldn't be the first time today," Wayne said.

"Yeah. Bobby told me about it." Gilbert stopped there, evidently too discreet to venture further.

"Did Bobby share the gory details?" Wayne asked. "Did he sound disappointed?"

Without answering the question directly, Gilbert said matter-of-factly, "It's time he outgrew his hero worship, boss. It was getting to be a burden for you."

"I knew there was a reason I hired you," Wayne said.

"It couldn't have been for my good looks." Gilbert mugged. "So—you want to talk about it—I mean about today?"

"No. That's why Eugene was here. To give me a lecture."

"Then that's taken care of." Gilbert changed the subject. "What are you doing still here? You've been off duty for hours."

"I was just thinking."

"About that kid?"

"Among other things," Wayne said. "I was wondering if he has a chance in hell."

"From what Bobby told me, you did your best by him with his parents."

"Well, I did get the family to admit there's a problem. One that money alone isn't going to solve."

Wayne's eyes met Gilbert's as he continued, "You know—it's a cliché, but I believe Mike was asking for help when he drew that gun. He'd done just about everything else to get his mother and father's attention. Then I came along and managed to make myself available."

"Next time," Gilbert said, "don't present such a tempting target."

Wayne chuckled. "Next time, I'll try to anticipate events."

"Since you're here," Gilbert said, "I want to talk to you about Tom, Zack's bartender. Although if you're leaving, it can wait.

"I wasn't. Have a seat and talk."

"Well, it isn't so much the bartender as it is his car. I keep seeing it at Zack's when the place is supposed to be closed and empty. Most of the time, the car's out of sight. But of course, I'm checking around back as per instructions. Struck me as odd that it would be there if he wasn't. Remember last Sunday?"

Wayne nodded. "Maybe Tom's doing double duty. Who does Zack hire to clean the bar while the place is closed to business? We need to question them."

"I have," Gilbert said, earning a satisfied nod of Wayne's head. "Tom works most nights. He mixes drinks and washes glasses, and that's the extent of it. Carmen and her sister do the cleaning every morning."

"Carmen?"

"The wife of one of the hands on the Double C Ranch. Now the interesting thing is that Carmen and her sister only clean the bar, the dance hall and the entertainers' dressing rooms. They're instructed to leave the rest alone. Zack keeps the other rooms locked up tighter than a drum."

"I'd sure give a lot for a look in those rooms," Wayne said.

"Well—we could get an insider to give us a hand."

"Who did you have in mind?" Wayne asked.

"Tiny maybe? Or Al or one of his band members?" Gilbert paused. "Or maybe Jessica Reynolds."

Wayne crossed his arms and stared hard at Gilbert. "Is this a fishing expedition?"

"Not when you look like that, it's not," Gilbert said fervently. A knock on the door made them both jump. Tiny entered at their invitation, and the two lawmen shared a speculative look.

"I thought you worked most evenings," Wayne said to Tiny after a mutual greeting.

"I do. But I got John Bob to cover for me. He works when I'm off. I told Zack my old lady was sick."

Gilbert and Wayne waited.

Tiny stared at his hands for a few seconds. "I told you Zack's been good to me," he said reluctantly.

Wayne nodded.

"But I think more than gambling is going on," Tiny said. "Zack asked me to stay late last night. Tom was there, too, and some guy I'd never met. Anyway—they had this big moving truck. And we loaded it in the dark. There wasn't even a moon. You couldn't hardly see your hand in front of your face."

Tiny looked at Wayne. "Now why would they load up a truck in the dark?"

"Good question," Wayne said. "What were they loading?"

"That's what really got me," Tiny said. "It's why I came to see you. Me and my old lady talked it over, and she agreed I should. When I saw you through the window, Sheriff, I came on in." The man paused, then added, "I think we were loading stolen goods, Sheriff Jackson."

"What kind of stolen goods?" Wayne asked.

"Most of it was boxed so I couldn't tell for sure. But I snuck a peek in one and I saw video equipment. Video equipment—would you believe? And not just ordinary VCRs. The one I saw was fancy-dancy. At the end, we loaded box after box of videotapes. I'd've never believed all that stuff was at Zack's."

"Do you have any idea when it was brought to Zack's in the first place?" Wayne asked, feeling a rush of adrenaline.

"No idea whatsoever." Tiny shook his head. "But I do know Zack's been paranoid the whole summer." He met Wayne's look with a new assurance. "And I can testify that those two characters you saw showed up for the first time around April or May."

"Very good, Tiny," Wayne said. "You and your wife were right to report this."

"I—I've never snitched on anybody before," Tiny said. "Zack's been good to me."

"He wasn't good to you when he involved you in a possible crime. And if you'd been convicted of a crime it would have involved your family."

"So you think it was stolen goods?"

"That or something close to it," Wayne said. "Did you help unload the boxes? Do you know where they ended up?"

"Nope. I don't think they trusted me enough for that."

"I'm not surprised. Listen—will you keep your eyes open for anything irregular? That's all we want."

"Okay," Tiny said.

"And if Zack asks you to do this again, do it and then report to us. Don't come by, just phone us. If you feel you're in any danger, contact us immediately."

"You think I'm in danger from Zack?" Tiny asked, flexing his biceps. "I can take care of him with one hand tied behind me."

Remembering his own experience, Wayne cautioned Tiny, "A bullet can kill you no matter how strong you are."

"Zack's never carried a gun," Tiny said. "He doesn't have the constitution for it."

"Maybe not," Wayne said. "But those other two characters are dangerous."

"Yeah." Tiny pondered Wayne's warning. "You're probably right. Listen—I can tell you one more thing. It might not mean anything, but Zack owns some land around Wimberley. I heard him say he'd bought it for investment reasons. Anyway, I'm telling you, for what it's worth.''

"Do you suspect they moved the goods there?" Wayne asked.

"No. Not really. I don't think there's even a house there. From what Zack said, it's just some land. I was thinking today of everything I know about Zack—I mean that you might call interesting. That's why I mentioned it.''

"Good thinking. If you remember anything else interesting, let us know. And thanks again for coming.''

Tiny paused at the door. "I had to—come, I mean. I thought about it a lot today. He's been such a jerk lately. Like hitting on Jessie. I couldn't stand by and let that happen. You understand, Sheriff?''

"Yes, Tiny, I do.''

AFTER TINY'S EXIT, the two men said nothing for a moment.

Finally Wayne gave out a gust of air that ended in a chuckle. "All in all, it's been quite a day. I guess we can forget about a search warrant for Zack's Place. I suspect it's clean as a whistle by now.''

"Yeah, but was it stolen goods or not?''

"Or is Zack involved in video piracy?''

"Zack doesn't have those kinds of connections. All he knows is music.''

"Stan Boozer and Maynard Kipling have those kinds of connections. I'll be real interested to hear what Lenny's found out." Wayne glanced at his watch. "He should be on duty. Maybe we'll catch him at his desk."

As he reached for the phone, it rang insistently and the button lit up his direct line. When he answered it, Jessie's shaken voice rushed into his ear.

"I just talked to Nora," she said. "She told me you almost got killed today."

It only took Wayne a moment to decide his call to Lenny could wait. "Nora exaggerated a little," he said soothingly. "Don't get upset."

He twisted his chair around to gesture that he didn't need company, but Gilbert had already gotten the message and closed the door between them.

The dusk had turned to night, and the only lamp Wayne had switched on in his office was the one used to illuminate his desk. Outside the pool of light, darkness obscured everything.

It added to the shared intimacy of the moment.

"What are you doing?" he asked, his voice growing husky.

"What do you mean what am I doing?" she replied, her voice strained. "I told you Nora called and told me you were almost shot. She says it's all over town."

"And Nora thought you ought to know."

His irony was wasted on Jessie right at that moment.

"I'm glad somebody called me." Accusation threaded her words.

"Nothing happened," Wayne said, wanting to dispense with the subject. "I subdued him immediately."

"What does 'subdued' mean?"

"I disarmed him," Wayne said patiently.

"You disarmed a druggie with a gun?"

"Look—" Wayne stared out the window "—why don't I come into Austin and you can yell at me in person?"

He heard her catch her breath. "Well—I was heading for the studio when Nora called. Patrick's waiting there for me."

"You go on to the studio. I'll meet you there. Where is it?"

She gave him the address.

"I'll see you in about an hour."

"Okay," she said reluctantly. "Are you sure you're all right?"

"I am now."

"Does this happen to you often?"

"Does what happen to me often?"

She huffed. "You know—almost getting shot."

Wayne examined the question from various angles, knowing that answering it would be a delicate matter.

"Well? Does it?" she asked insistently.

"Not very often."

"Once a day? Once a year? Should I expect calls like this from Nora?"

What she said and the way she said it made Wayne's head swim.

"I'll tell you what," he said. "I'll call you next time as soon as it happens. That way you won't have to hear it from Nora."

"Well—I guess that'll have to do." Her voice dropped to a whisper. "But hurry. I want to see for myself that you're in one piece."

CHAPTER TEN

SHE KNEW he was there. It was scary how she always could sense him. Swiveling around on her stool, Jessie found Wayne propped against a wall, an enigmatic look masking his features. She'd been afraid she'd be embarrassed to meet him as his lover. But she was so happy to see him whole and healthy that she forgot to be self-conscious.

"I didn't hear you come in." She slid off her perch, needing to touch him.

"No, don't let me interrupt," he said, moving toward her with those impossibly long strides, picking her up around her waist and setting her on the stool again, his grasp lingering for a moment. "I'm enjoying finding out how a song gets put together. Hello—" He held out a hand to Patrick. "I'm Wayne Jackson."

And this woman's taken. Wayne couldn't have made it plainer if he'd spoken it aloud.

Patrick cocked a brow at Jessie before returning the handshake. "Patrick Lane at your service. We're just putting together some instrumentations. They can wait."

"No need for that. I'll make myself comfortable. I saw a pot of coffee in one of the rooms."

"Please, help yourself," Patrick offered.

"I could also use a phone, if you've got one handy."

"Is Claudia here? She can show you where one is."

"Well, if it's not the lawman." Claudia's simpering voice announced her entrance. She smiled sweetly at Jessie. "I'll entertain Sheriff Jackson while you two work." Turning to him, she lowered her lashes. "I'd be glad for you to use my phone. It's right through here."

"I could also use a sandwich," Wayne said mildly, "if you'll point me in the direction of a deli."

"I know just the place," Claudia said and drew him from the room.

Patrick's lips twitching, he said to Jessie, "So that's your sheriff. Claudia doesn't usually throw her bait into such deep waters."

"All she can see is his muscles," Jessie said with a scowl.

"You'll have to admit they're hard to ignore."

Jessie shook her head. "He's so much more than machismo and muscles."

"How do you see him, Jess?"

"As kind but decisive and very self-contained." She halted when she heard what she'd revealed to herself. "I guess I only see what he's willing to show me."

"Do you know what I'm seeing?"

She shook her head.

"A different woman from the one I've known. You're vulnerable to him in a way I've never seen you."

"It happens to the best of us." As soon as she said it, she realized her remark had emerged as bleak rather than flippant.

Patrick took a moment to study her. "Is this where I assume my best-friend role and remind you to be careful?"

Looking away, she admitted with chagrin, "Neither of us was thinking the other night."

"Oh, that's great." He felt around in his pockets. "Wait—let me get out my lecture on safe sex."

"That's not what I mean," she said forlornly. "Anyway, this relationship's hazardous under any conditions."

"Okay." He thought for a second. "I'll print out a label you can slap on his backside. Warning—this man could hurt a woman badly."

She giggled before her face grew somber. "He's already hurt me. He doesn't want to be involved. He wouldn't if he could help himself."

"Hmmm." Patrick tutted softly. "Sounds to me like you're in way too deep."

"Up to my eyeballs."

"Then you'd better find a way to protect your heart, honey chile."

"My armor melted on Tuesday."

"Well, then—there's nothing more for me to say. Except—it's better to have loved and lost than never to have loved at all, because a broken heart gives you more things to write about. I figure this affair will be good for at least two songs."

"You're a horrible, horrible man," Jessie said, somewhere between tears and laughter. She elbowed him, and he toppled from his stool into a heap.

"Are you hurt?" she asked, momentarily anxious.

He picked himself up and examined his limbs for injury. "I didn't know being a best friend could be hazardous to my health."

"Idiot," she said, grateful that he'd lightened the moment. "Look—" she pointed to the orchestrated score he'd printed from his computer screen "—I want the melody to echo me throughout the third repeat."

Surprisingly, they got back to work with ease, and Jessie realized that it had been cathartic to admit that the affair with Wayne was potentially heart-shattering. Her mood had been volatile since she'd received the call from Nora. Talking to Patrick had given her a certain kind of peace.

Thirty minutes later, she felt a tingle between her shoulder blades. This time it didn't make her tense, just physically aware. She glanced around and found Wayne thoughtfully munching a sandwich. Claudia, she was pleased to see, was nowhere in sight.

"I'll just be another minute or two," Jessie said.

"Don't hurry," Wayne instructed her. "I'm still eating. I have another one of these." He waved his sandwich at her.

Good Lord, if they ever lived together, he'd eat her out of house and home.

"You look hot," Patrick said, putting his palm to her forehead. "I hope you're not catching anything." The concern in his voice was definitely overdone.

The look she sent made him reel in mock fear as though he were about to fall off his stool again.

"I think we've come to a stopping point," Jessie said.

Wayne polished off the sandwich, wiped his fingers carefully, strolled over and planted a quick kiss on her lips.

"See," he said. "I'm fine. Not a nick on me." He moved away and held out his arms. "You can take a closer look if you want."

"Later—" She flushed.

That drew a sexy grin that sent her pulse rate way up.

"I thought you'd be at Kickers by now," he said.

"They're trying out a new act. I don't go on until after midnight."

"Christ," he said, "this work has horrible hours."

"I also work Christmas and New Year." She felt required to point this out to him.

"We'll see about that," he said to himself more than to anybody else. He took her arm. "Are you ready to go?"

"Yes."

They waved goodbye to an amused Patrick and went out into the dusk.

As soon as they were alone, Jessie threw her arms around Wayne, for the first time allowing herself the luxury of expressing her feelings.

"Hey—what's this all about?" he asked, returning her hug. "I said I was fine."

"Ever since Nora called me," she said into his chest, "I've been remembering how Lenny looked with blood all over him. I kept thinking about you, imagining you—" Her voice caught.

"I'm sorry." He kissed the top of her head through her tangle of curls. "I forgot what you'd been through." He pulled away to grin at her. "But you shouldn't worry. Lenny and I don't hang around with the same company. I've got better taste."

She laughed shakily.

"That's better." He kissed her on the mouth in swift reassurance. "Now where's your car?"

"I rode my bicycle over." She pointed out an ancient five-speed. "It's only ten blocks to my place."

She watched his expression cloud over.

"You ride your bike at night in this neighborhood?" Even as he asked the question, he loaded the bike into the back of his truck.

"I do it all the time."

''That doesn't make it sensible.''

''Sensible is not my claim to fame.''

Catching her hand, he swung her so that they were facing each other. ''What is your claim to fame?'' he asked, his eyes glinting.

Her heart thumping noisily, she lowered her lashes and whispered, ''Come up to my place and I'll show you.''

Something suspiciously like a growl came from deep in his throat. His hands tightened and then began stroking her arms.

''In the meantime—'' he kissed her cheek ever so lightly ''—will you drive your car to the studio from now on—at night—for me?''

As she gazed into his eyes, she recognized the same anxiety she'd felt around his misadventure.

''Yes,'' she said softly. ''I'll only ride my bike during the daytime.''

''Thank you,'' he said. This time he lazily covered her mouth with his. The contact flashed out of control before either of them expected.

''I was wondering,'' she breathed, ''when you were going to get around to an honest-to-God kiss.''

''I didn't think an honest-to-God kiss was wise. It's been all I could do not to haul you away from here.''

''You told me to go on working.''

By this time, they'd had climbed into the truck, and Wayne had started the engine. As he pulled away from the curb he said, ''I liked watching you work.''

"You did? What about the time—?" She stopped, appalled that she'd landed them in the middle of a touchy subject.

"You mean the time you left me and went into the living room and tried to pretend I didn't exist."

"That's not—I didn't—how did you know?"

"I knew."

"So that's the reason you made love to me like—"

"I wanted to get your attention."

"You did that all right."

There was silence between them for the next several moments. Not a tense quietude but a tentative one.

When they arrived at the apartment, Mrs. Peters was in her yard, and Jessie knew she had to introduce Wayne.

"Mrs. Peters, I'd like you to meet Wayne Jackson, a friend of mine. This is my landlady, Mrs. Peters."

"How do you do." Wayne smiled down into the woman's face.

"Are you a singer like Jessie?" she asked, as though she had the question ready.

"Oh, no." Wayne laughed. "I'm just a cop."

"A cop?" The elderly woman's expression widened.

"Wayne is sheriff of Claro County," Jessie explained.

"Well—" Mrs. Peters smiled, her satisfaction evident "—I'm very glad to meet you, Sheriff Jackson. It's nice to know Jessie has someone steady to look after her."

Jessie had been afraid this would happen. "I'm sorry we can't stay and chat, Mrs. Peters." She hurried toward the stairs, dragging Wayne behind her. "I have something I need to do—" A lame excuse if she'd ever heard one.

But Mrs. Peters went along, a knowing expression on her face. "Don't let me keep you," she called. "I know you must be busy."

"I believe you've made a conquest," Jessie said sotto voce to Wayne as she unlocked her door.

"We're trained to be nice to everyone."

"Everyone?"

As soon as they were inside, he gathered her close. "What do you think?"

"I think I'll wait and see."

"When do you have to be at Kickers?" he asked against her cheek.

"Not for a while."

"Good. Then you won't have to wait." He kissed her cheek. "Do you realize you made me forget my other sandwich?"

Something about his accusation made Jessie giggle. Smothered laughter got in the way of her speech. "M-maybe—Patrick will f-find it and eat it."

"What's so funny?" He swept her off her feet with a single motion.

"Has anyone ever told you, you eat like a horse?" She draped her arms around his neck, feeling glorious all of a sudden.

"I have to keep up my energy." He grinned. "Especially lately."

She glanced at him demurely. "You'll have to get in better shape."

"What shape would you like me?" His tone was amused, but his look was sultry.

"Any way I can get you," she said in a rush.

By this time, they'd reached the bed and both collapsed on it.

"I think that can be arranged." He covered her mouth with his.

They didn't start hot and heavy, but they headed that way fast. And each was impatient with the other's clothing.

Once they were skin to skin, Wayne slowed down.

Rolling to his back, he had her straddle his hips. "That's better," he said. "Now I can take a look at you."

He studied her breasts as if they were pearls, turning her torso to the lamplight. In the soft illumination her skin glowed a creamy white. He ran his hands over her skin, tracing the faint blue veins that lay beneath it. Trailing the color that seeped up her throat.

She'd never been handled with such tender loving care. Each time they made love he worshiped her body.

Taking each nipple, he worried them gently. All the while, his expression was intent. He seemed content to drive her crazy.

She couldn't stand it any longer and bent so that her nipples brushed his lips.

"What do you want?" He gave her a single lick of his tongue.

"More," she whispered.

He licked the other breast.

"More," she gasped.

He took a nipple into his mouth and drew on it slowly.

"More..." She slipped down his body and enveloped him.

"Wait," he groaned and had to pull away. "Damn it, woman—you don't leave a man room to navigate."

"Huh?"

"You want to do the honors?" He offered her the packet.

By the time she had the condom on securely, they were both hot and bothered.

"Now then, where were we?"

The question was rhetorical, Jessie discovered, because before she could answer, he had her astride him.

This time he was the one to ease her hips down until he nestled against her entrance. When he slipped inside, both of them quivered with delight.

"Am I ever going to be able to go slow with you the first time?" he wondered.

"I don't know. I can't seem to go slow either."

"Then let's go fast and catch up later."

"I think...I think that's an...an excellent idea. Ohhh—oh me..."

"What's the matter, little darlin'?"

She rode him hard, and the words came out in puffs. "You know...what's...the matter... because...you're...doing it to me. Ahhhhh..."

He plunged deep, and she collapsed, throbbing around him.

He came with a smothered cry, his breath hot against her breast.

"You know," he said after a long five minutes, "one of these days we might get the hang of this."

Maybe it was the drawl, maybe it was his conjecture. Maybe it was the sexual release, the silky feeling of repletion.

Whatever it was, she began to laugh.

"Now what's funny?" He nipped at her breast.

"You. Sometimes you say these ridiculous things in a drawling kind of way like you're not sure you're going to make it from the beginning to the end of the sentence. And it just strikes me as funny."

"It doesn't take much to amuse you," he said indulgently.

"Oh, come on. You mean for me to laugh." She gave him a playful punch in his side.

"Wooooph," he grunted as though she'd dealt him a lethal blow.

"Oh, yeah, sure. I guess I've found a weak spot." She tried tickling him. "Have I discovered your Achilles' heel?"

"You're my Achilles' heel." He caught her arms to her sides so that she couldn't get at him.

"Funny—" she batted her eyelashes "—I don't feel like a heel."

He nuzzled her throat. "You don't look like one either."

"I'd rather be Delilah. You be Samson."

"I'd look pretty silly," he drawled, "with hair down to my badge."

The image he brought to mind sent Jessie off into another fit of giggles. "Oh, my," she finally got out, "I didn't think there'd be laughter."

With an intake of breath, she stopped to hear what she'd just said. "I mean—" she hesitated "—after the other night I expected drama and tears and—and overwhelming passion. But I didn't expect—comedy. I didn't think we'd be able to laugh together."

She circled the thought, examining it closely. "You know what it is?" Her eyes met his.

"Why don't you tell me?"

"This is the first time I've ever been comfortable around you. I mean bone-lazy-don't-give-a-hoot-what-the-hell comfortable."

"You make me sound more like a house slipper than your lover," he grumbled.

"Do you think," she asked, "that between us we might have a foot fetish?"

"I don't know what you're talking about," he responded mildly before flipping her to her back from where she'd been perched on his stomach.

She was still wondering what was happening when he took one of her feet and began nibbling the big toe.

"You—you idiot!" Taking a pillow and whopping him with it, she tried to free her leg from his clutches. "You don't play fair, you big galoot." She hit him harder with the pillow.

"I think," he said, grunting, "the pillows are going to have to go." He threw both weapons on the floor and captured her beneath him.

Laughing up into his face, she saw a wave of tenderness wash over him.

"You didn't expect it, either," she whispered. "You didn't know we could have this."

"No. I didn't." His look flickered. "I wasn't sure what to expect."

"Admit it. I relax you."

He smiled down at her. "You're better than a hot tub."

When he eased his hold, she reached up to stroke his face.

"Do you know," she asked softly, "that I can always tell when you're close by? It's like a sixth sense. I knew before I saw you at the studio that you'd been there listening. Did you mean what you said about watching me work? I thought—"

"I know what you thought. That I resented your singing. If I did, I don't now. It was exciting to watch you and Patrick put the words and music together. You're an impressive team. I'm a little in awe of you."

"Then you don't begrudge—"

"I can't. Your talent's too big. Jessie—" His tone changed. "I don't want you to think I compare you to Michelle in any way."

Once he'd opened the subject, Jessie didn't mean to miss the opportunity. "Could you tell me about her? More about why it didn't work out between you?"

"Neither one of us knew how to make a marriage last. She'd never lived with a permanent family any more than I had. Her alcoholic grandmother raised her until she got too difficult to handle. We'd both spent our childhoods in group homes."

"I see what you mean."

He sighed at the remembrance. "We were like lost souls reaching out for each other. But we found out each other wasn't enough. Then she got stars in her eyes. Living in Las Vegas can do that to a person. When I dropped out of pro ball, she felt like I'd betrayed her ambitions. She'd hoped that being my wife . . ." His voice trailed away.

"Does it still bother you that I'm in the entertainment business?" Jessie asked with more understanding of why he was bitter.

"Yes. But not for the reason you think. The entertainment business isn't healthy, Jessie. I've seen it hurt people badly."

"I know that, Wayne."

"It's filled with drugs, alcohol and too much money. Gigantic egos, fragile personalities and pea-sized minds."

"I know. I know," she said, feeling on the defensive.

"Look," he said, "I don't want to talk about the business." Rolling onto his back, he pulled her on top of him. "We've got better things to do. I want to talk about you."

"There's not a lot to tell," she said, relaxing her head on his shoulder.

"How do your folks feel about your singing? Don't they worry about you?"

"Sure," she said. "That's what parents are for." Remembering his background, she tensed at her thoughtlessness.

"Don't," he said, massaging her spine. "Don't feel you have to guard your words. I wouldn't have asked if I hadn't wanted to hear about your family."

As Jessie lay there so close to him, understanding him in a way she hadn't before, she began to have an idea of the kinds of things he might want to hear.

"Do you know," she confided, "my mom and dad live in the same house they moved into when they were married? My great-grandparents' house, built in 1925. Granddad Reynolds deeded it to them as a wedding present. The floors sag and there's not enough closet space and Dad had to jerry-rig a second bathroom when the three of us were teenagers."

Jessie settled herself against Wayne more securely. "Dad wants to build Mom a new house but she says she doesn't need it. Especially now that there's just the two of them. I'm secretly glad."

"Why?"

"I love that old house. It's painted white with yellow trim. It has a picket fence, a porch and beds of roses in the yard. Mom's spent a thousand hours over those roses. They don't grow well in Monroe, but that never stopped her."

"She sounds as determined as her daughter."

"Yeah, I suspect I take after her. I couldn't have admitted that very long ago."

"And your dad?"

"The two boys take after him. He's deliberate and solid. You can always depend on him. You remind me a lot of him." She paused to consider what she'd said.

After a few seconds, she continued. "You ought to see his store. It looks just the way it did when my granddad opened it. On the side of the building, painted right on the bricks, is a faded advertisement for Gladiola Flour. The place has got all kinds of nooks and crannies filled with dusty fittings and gadgets that go back forty, fifty, even sixty years ago. And Dad, even Lee, can explain what they're used for. That's why they haven't lost business to the discount hardware stores. People in Monroe know who they can trust to know what they're doing.''

''Who's Lee?''

''My older brother. He became a partner a couple of years ago.''

''And your other brother?''

''Andy? He teaches math at Monroe Junior High. He's engaged to the history teacher.''

''So everyone but you stuck close to home.''

''Yeah. They're all just as happy as bugs in a rug. I never understood it. Monroe, Louisiana, wasn't big enough for me.''

''I can believe that.''

''Don't get me wrong,'' she protested. ''I love my hometown and I really miss my family. I don't know what I'd do if they didn't worry about me.''

When she paused to think, he didn't interrupt her.

''The fact of the matter is,'' she said, ''my parents didn't know what to do with me. Nobody else in the family even has red hair. Except for a great-aunt who ran away to New Orleans when she was sixteen and married a merchant marine. I guess that's who I take after. My great-aunt, I mean.''

''What did they say when you told them you wanted to be a singer?''

"They've known I wanted to sing ever since I asked Santa for a Patsy Cline album. I must have been all of seven years old. There was this pipe sticking up—I think it used to be part of a handrail. Anyway, it was just stuck there by the porch steps for years. That became my microphone. I'd give concerts to the neighborhood kids. Charged them a penny. You could say I went professional at an early age."

His soft chuckle reverberated through her. Her instincts had been right. This was what he wanted to hear.

"Later," she said, "I hooked up with some area bands. My dad didn't like that. Especially since the guys were usually older."

"Your poor dad," Wayne said with heartfelt sympathy.

"I know. It was hard on him. But he always loved to hear me sing. When I was a senior in high school and played the lead in *Bye Bye Birdie,* Mom and Dad came to every performance. Their support helped me develop the self-confidence I needed."

"I know that feeling." Wayne's tone was warm. "Harry and Charlene came to every one of my high school games."

She raised her head to stare at him. "Who are they?"

"The closest thing I have to family," he said, dumbfounding her. "He's the cop who arrested me for shoplifting when I was fourteen."

Jessie pulled away from him and rocked back on her haunches. When he didn't continue, she prodded, "Go on."

"There's not much to tell."

Only a man would say that, Jessie thought as she fought her frustration. Jessie crossed her arms like a schoolmarm, and earned a glinting grin from Wayne.

"I like that pose," he said, inspecting her. "It's sort of early Marilyn or late Madonna. I can just see your nipple peeking out—"

"That's enough," Jessie said sternly. "You're not changing the subject. Tell me about Harry and Charlene."

Resigned to the inevitable, he began to talk. "Harry took an interest in me. That's about the size of it. He believed I was salvageable when the odds weren't very good. He brought me into his home. Charlene practically adopted me. Harry's the one who steered me into football."

"Were you already big?"

"When Harry got hold of me, I was six feet tall, one hundred fifty pounds and all arms and legs."

Taking a small detour, she ran her hands up his torso. "You've filled out nicely."

When he reached for her, she evaded him.

"Talk," she directed.

"About what?"

"Football," she decided.

"You can thank football for about seventy pounds. It also kept me in school and out of mischief. When I started playing I began to believe in myself. Harry and my coach helped me get an athletic scholarship. That's what put me through college.''

"And then you went to the pros."

"Yeah, but the NFL was always just a detour. The glamorous life never appealed to me like it did to Michelle.''

"I guess Harry's the reason you became a cop.''

"He never said he wanted me to follow in his footsteps. He didn't expect Bobby, his son, to become one, either, but that's the way it happened. Right now, Bobby's working as one of my deputies.''

"Is Bobby the deputy who needs to keep his pants on?''

"Yeah. And now look at me. I'm one to be talking.''

"I don't know what you mean.'' She settled herself beside him again, letting her hand wander over his chest. "Why would you want to wear your pants in bed?''

She loved it when his laughter rippled through her body. He gathered her close, and she expected his hands to do some roaming of their own.

He surprised her when he returned to an earlier subject. "Did you start singing full-time as soon as you left high school?''

"I went to college for a year. I promised my folks I'd do that. But I knew right away that college wasn't where I belonged. All my mom and dad ever wanted was for me to be happy. And they understood enough to realize that I'd have to find my way there.''

''Are you happy?''

She didn't answer right away. ''That's a broad question.''

''Right at this moment—'' He narrowed it down.

She snuggled closer. ''Yes, I am.''

''Were you happy before we met?''

''Yes. For the most part. Maybe not like this. I mean—maybe not as in right-at-this-moment-no-other-moment-counting kind of way. Except when I'm singing.''

''You make love to your songs the same way you make love with me. Did you realize that?''

''No.''

''That's what shook me the first time I saw you. Your passion. It seized me and shook me like I've never been shaken.'' When he found her lips, she felt him tremble. Or was it herself rocked by the passion he explored?

Now his hands began to memorize her body. Just as her hands learned the contours of his.

They made love slowly this time, taking care with each other, their caresses almost reverential. As if they were in awe of the emotions they evoked. And even toward the last when they were lost in each other, their dance of love was like a dreamy waltz.

How many ways were there to make love? Jessie wondered as she lay sated beside him.

GUITARS, CADILLACS

"Oh, God—" when he finally spoke, his voice was raspy "—you're right. This is like nothing I've ever felt before."

Underlying his words, she heard the wonder and the fear.

CHAPTER ELEVEN

JESSIE AND WAYNE were eating lunch in the Long-horn Coffee Shop on a Monday afternoon in late August. Actually, right at this moment, Jessie was doing more talking than eating, since Nora had stopped by the table to visit.

This was the third weekend in a row Jessie had come to Crystal Creek.

Wayne amended his mental arithmetic. For the third weekend in a row he'd traveled to Austin to get her Sunday afternoon and returned her to her apartment early Tuesday morning. He hadn't given her much choice in the arrangements.

She interrupted her chat with Nora to give him a quick, tender smile, which told him she recognized his reluctance to participate in a female discussion. The understanding they shared shook him as always. Already they had a lovers' language of their own.

Neither of them had much choice in this headlong relationship. If Wayne knew anything, it was that they were both in over their heads.

Thoughtfully chewing a cottage fry, he leaned back in the booth, careful not to accidentally brush her leg under the table. Any physical contact sent their senses spiraling, and this was one time he wanted to be detached. In fact, it became a challenge to observe Jessie with a degree of objectivity. Wearing baggy shorts and T-shirt, she looked about as glamorous as a Cabbage Patch doll.

Right now she and Nora were discussing the price of hot dogs, having already covered Rory's baseball career and the Little League game scheduled for later that evening. As they talked, Wayne could clearly discern the down-to-earth gal from Monroe, Louisiana.

Then the sunlight through the window caught her flame-red hair. Her cat-green eyes sparkled with humor. The exquisite lines of her cheekbones hollowed out shadows, her generous mouth curved into a smile over white, even teeth. And Wayne was reminded with a jolt that the woman seated across from him was a world-class beauty.

He understood better why she downplayed her looks offstage. Such near perfection could get in the way of friendships.

When she gestured extravagantly, and her throaty laugh bubbled up, and her voice caught with a husky intensity, before Wayne's eyes appeared the spellbinding performer.

She absently smoothed her fingers along her arm, and he felt the touch of his ardent lover.

She was all these women and more. A disciplined professional. A soft touch with animals. Vulnerable in ways he couldn't have imagined.

There wasn't a manipulative bone in Jessie's body. In fact, he thought she was too honest and forthright for her own good. Especially in the world she inhabited.

But that was one of the subjects they couldn't discuss. Zack's name hadn't come up between them once in the past three weeks. Neither had they mentioned Todd nor the tour Wayne knew was coming.

They were holding on to each moment as hard as they could. But Wayne realized with a chill that the future was gaining. And he wasn't even sure they could face it together.

"Hey—" Jessie nudged him gently. "Don't tell me you've gone to sleep without finishing your hamburger. I'll get scared you're sick or something."

He looked around and noticed Nora's absence. Glancing down at his half-full plate he realized he'd forgotten his meal.

"I guess I'm too tuckered out to eat," he murmured, a single finger prodding hers. "Some wild woman kept me up half the night moaning and groaning."

"Hush," Jessie said with a glare, jerking her hand out of reach. "Remember where we are. We draw enough stares as it is. And you'd better eat. You'll need all your strength to coach the kids tonight."

He didn't respond immediately. Instead, he just sat there with an odd smile on his face.

"What?" she asked, blushing and not sure why. "Why are you looking at me like that?"

"You know, the stares we get are nothing compared to what people are saying."

"I probably know what they're saying better than you. Do they think their clean-living, do-gooding sheriff's been seduced by a wicked, wayward woman?"

He decided on candor. "They're saying it's about time a lady turned the stuffy, stiff-necked sheriff's head."

Her grin was satisfied and a little smug. Anyone watching them would have had a good idea about the nature of the conversation, even though they were both speaking quietly enough so that no one could hear.

"Wayne—"

He turned at the sound of Gilbert's voice and found his deputy standing beside the table.

"I hoped I'd catch up with you here," Gilbert said. "Hello, Ms. Reynolds." He nodded to Jessie. "I bought your new CD. It's great."

"Call me Jessie, please. I didn't know you were a fan of country music."

"I have been ever since I heard you sing the first time."

"Thank you. That's a very nice compliment."

She turned her smile on Gilbert, and his eyes glazed over.

Wayne cleared his throat. "What do you need?"

"Oh." Gilbert pulled himself together. "I wondered if I could talk to you, boss. Something's come up—" His look touched Jessie before returning to Wayne. "Maybe you could come over to the office for a few minutes."

Wayne glanced Jessie's way in question.

"Go on," she said. "I'll run over to Miller's Department Store. I need another pair of Levi's, and it's nice not to have to fight Austin crowds."

"Come to the office when you're finished," he said and lightly ran his hand along her upper arm. It was the merest gesture of farewell, but her eyes fluttered shut in unconscious reaction.

It was holy hell for both of them being in public, Wayne decided as he and Gilbert crossed the street to the courthouse.

An X-rated couple in a PG world.

"Why the grimace?" Gilbert asked as they entered the office.

Wayne shook his head in dismissal, and Gilbert was wise enough not to repeat the question.

Instead, he apologized. "I'm sorry I took you away from Jessie on your day off."

"Don't worry about it. I'm dragging her to the game later. What did you want to tell me?"

"It's about Zack. I didn't think you'd want to discuss him—in front of—I mean, in the café."

"You're right. What have you found out?"

"We finally got an answer on his Wimberley property. It took this long because their records aren't computerized."

Wayne nodded encouragement.

"He did own ten acres outside the city limits."

"Did?" Wayne's brow shot up.

"According to the deed he sold it to a company called—" Gilbert glanced down at his notes "—Southwestern Bar and Billiard."

"When?"

"Four months ago. Just after Boozer and Kipling came on the scene."

"What have you found out about Southwestern Bar and Billiard?"

"The address given is in Dallas. But I haven't been able to track it down. The whole setup feels phony."

"I wonder what anyone would want with a patch of rocky Texas soil? The land around Wimberley doesn't grow anything but goats and cacti. How does the deed describe the property?"

"As undeveloped and unused. There's no structure or livestock and no water or electricity."

"And no way we can get a search warrant to find out for sure what's there. Not if Zack no longer owns it." Wayne thought for a moment. "Have you checked county records within the area to see if he's bought other acreage?"

Gilbert nodded. "This is the only land we could connect with Zack outside of the dance hall. He has a mortgage on that of a hundred and fifty thousand dollars.''

''Okay. Get hold of Lenny. See if he's found out any more about Boozer's activities. The last two times we've talked, he didn't have anything to report. But now we've got this company—Southwestern Bar and Billiard. The two may link up. I told him about the midnight move, and he's real interested in knowing more of Zack's activities.''

Wayne and Gilbert looked at each other speculatively.

''I tell you what,'' Wayne said after a minute. ''I think it's time we got a search warrant for Zack's Place. If we point to the links between Zack, Boozer, pirated videos or stolen VCRs, I think the judge will come through with one.''

''We won't find anything when we search it.''

''Probably not. But I bet we scare the hell out of Zack. Maybe if we rattle him enough he'll make a mistake. It'll only take one.''

''And then we'll have him.''

Wayne's expression hardened. ''Getting Zack isn't enough. I want Boozer and Kipling. They've ruined a lot of lives.''

''You really hate gambling, don't you?''

''My ex-wife's a compulsive gambler. She can't break away from it.''

''I see. Then here's to collaring Kipling and Boozer.''

Wayne's smile was wolfish. "I have a feeling they've already made their mistake. I think that dummy company's a front for their activities. They're going to be real sorry they tried to move into Texas."

Watching his boss's glittering expression, Gilbert was sure Wayne spoke the truth.

"COME ON, Tigers! Come on, we need a hit!"

"Throw it over the plate. Strike him out, Scotty!"

"Come on, Rory! Hit a home run! You can do it!"

"Strike three? You're kidding! Get your glasses checked, Ump!" Nora's voice stood out over all the others, probably because she was sitting by Jessie, directly behind home plate.

The official, who Nora said taught Sunday school, gave her a go-to-hell look before returning to his duties.

Jessie choked back a chuckle and pulled Nora down beside her on the splintery bench.

"Cool off, Nora," she said. "We've got three innings to rally."

"Not with those calls," Nora said loudly. "The man can't see."

"But he can hear," Jessie whispered. "And he's going to banish us to the fence if you don't calm down."

Nora looked a little sheepish. "I get carried away sometimes." Grinning, she added, "But you'll notice I'm not as bad as Ken."

This was true.

The umpire had already ejected Ken Slattery from the bleachers. He was standing near the dugout watching Rory's team, the Tigers, fan out onto the field.

This was the third Monday Jessie had gone to the Little League ballpark to watch the Tigers play ball. To watch Wayne coach them. To cheer them on by Nora's side.

The team had already won the city championship. Now they were playing in a Tri-County Tournament. Unfortunately, the Johnson City Wildcats were whipping them ten to two.

Sitting here in the gathering dusk with the heat of the day gradually fading, Jessie could almost believe she was a girl again. She'd been a Little League Princess the summer she'd turned ten years old. The Reynolds Plumbing Supply Bear Cubs had chosen her. It had been quite an honor.

She'd raised eight hundred dollars selling chocolate pecan bars. But Kitty Savoy had sold twelve hundred dollars worth. Kitty had been crowned queen, and Jessie had been crushed.

Remembering the past brought resonance to the present. She looked all around her, gathering in the sensations.

The dust and fireflies. The canned sodas and snow cones. Cheering parents letting go of their inhibitions.

The smell of young sweat, crushed grass and hot popcorn. The occasional whiff of cigar smoke.

Everything conspired to make her dangerously vulnerable. She'd always been a sucker for a Little League game.

During these magic hours in the twilight, she'd seen that nothing mattered more to Wayne than these kids.

He always squatted down to talk to them. She'd yet to see him criticize one of them for a mistake, although they always came to him after they'd committed an error.

Right now, Wayne was illustrating a throwing technique to the losing pitcher. The other team had already pounded him for thirteen hits. After a while, Wayne rubbed the boy's shoulder and whispered something in his ear. The child flashed him a watery grin.

It was more than Jessie could handle. She blinked her eyes to clear them and was afraid she might have to escape behind the bleachers before Nora noticed she'd been moved to tears by a pitching lesson.

Would Wayne be like this with his own son? With *their* son?

The realization hit her like a splash of cold water, and goose bumps rose on her bare arms and legs.

She was in love with Wayne, and she wanted his baby.

Nora looked her way curiously.

Jessie shook her head, sure that she wore a stricken expression.

How could she have been so stupid as to fall in love? When had she had any choice in the matter? It had started approximately two seconds after he had loomed over Zack's shoulder, long before she could have worked up an immunity.

She'd been denying the obvious from the moment they'd met.

"Jessie, are you okay?" Nora asked. "You've been staring into space for the past twenty minutes. The other team's gotten three more runs off us. I'm not sure we can take two more innings."

The Tigers rallied, however, in the fifth, sixth and seventh, and they lost the game by a respectable 16–10.

Jessie did what she could to follow the action, but she kept wondering how she would greet Wayne afterward. She wondered if her new knowledge was written on her face.

Once the game had ended, the players gathered around him to be led in a final cheer by Roy, his assistant. They were joined by clumps of parents, consoling each other for tonight's loss, but congratulating themselves on a winning season, and talking up next summer's prospects. Jessie stood back by the fence, happy to be ignored.

The crowd had thinned out considerably by the time Wayne reached her.

"I hope you don't mind," he began. "We're going out for one last pizza. I can't get out of it. You don't have to come."

"Don't be silly," she said. "Besides, you haven't fed me supper."

"I have to admit, several of the boys would like to meet you." He lowered his voice, "Not to mention their parents."

"Just as long as I don't have to eat anchovies."

"Would I make you do such thing? I insist on buying you your very own pizza."

"Sure, so you don't have to share one. You're a prince of a guy."

That was the extent of their conversation for the rest of the evening. And Jessie was relieved, for once, to be surrounded by a crowd.

A nice, average crowd of giggling kids and joking parents. Average families with average dreams and average problems.

These people lived in a different world from the one Jessie inhabited. She hadn't remembered how relaxing it felt to be in that other world again.

For the first time, she really understood what she'd been missing.

Becoming a singer had been a self-absorbing task. She had been the instrument of her own achievement. Her face, her body, her voice, her talent, her soul to be explored and disciplined. She'd had to view herself with a determined objectivity. She'd also had to be her strongest critic and staunchest fan.

Jessie guessed writers and actors faced the same problem, the inner obsessiveness and self-direction. For ten years she hadn't had a life outside her goals. Those goals had given her direction and deep satisfaction and an exhilaration she knew she could never give up.

But the people around her this night had more important things to worry about than the next performance. They had spouses and children to love and fret about. Homes to make and take care of. Jobs to do. They couldn't wrap themselves in their inner goals and personalities. They didn't have time to continually take their emotional pulse.

As Wayne drove her back to his house late in the evening, Jessie felt as though she were caught in the nether regions, not belonging to his world or hers. Not knowing whether either one could satisfy her, now that she'd tasted the joys of both.

She loved Wayne, he was profoundly important to her, but their lives would inevitably diverge, and she felt when that happened she'd be torn in two.

They didn't have enough time. Her watch said ten o'clock when he pulled into his driveway. They had to leave for Austin by six-thirty the next morning so Wayne could drive back to Crystal Creek in time for work.

"Tired?" he asked as they walked to the front door. "You haven't said anything for the past ten minutes."

"A little," she said.

After they went inside, he put his arm around her and led her to the bedroom.

Stretching her arm around his waist, she tried to keep it light. "Yelling your head off can be hard work. I'm sure you must be tired from coaching."

"Not really. It's one of the most enjoyable things I do."

As opposed to dealing with crime and criminals, the career that had molded him. He obviously loved his work with the children. And suddenly she understood one of the reasons why. Both jobs gave him the chance she didn't have to be outwardly focused.

"Has Crystal Creek thought about starting a football league, since that's your specialty?"

"We decided the town wasn't big enough to support it. But I'm a consultant to the junior and senior high school programs."

He'd made the conscious effort to become a part of this town. He would never leave. She'd never ask him.

"What was that about?" he asked.

"What?"

"The look on your face." He lifted her chin. "The sadness."

She shook her head. "It's just that we never have enough time."

He gathered her into his arms. "I'm sorry about tonight."

"That's not what I meant. I love watching you with the kids," she confessed. "You're so kind and supportive."

"I learned that from Harry. He's a cop, but he's one of the gentlest men I know. He taught me that to help people you have to learn to bring out their best."

She clung to him, afraid that she might crumble into a million pieces.

"What's wrong?" he asked, his voice concerned.

"Nothing. I don't know."

But she did.

She loved this man deeply. She loved everything he stood for. Yet she wasn't sure how their relationship could possibly last.

"Just hold me," she said.

"It's okay," he soothed her as he might a tearful child. "It's okay." He stroked her back and arms, then cradled her head in his fingers. "I'm here." He kissed her slowly and softly.

She wanted more.

Before she'd ever met him, she'd escaped unhappiness by losing herself in her music. Now she wanted to lose herself in him.

Dragging his head down to hers, she kissed him with a desperate intensity, biting and nipping his lips and tongue. Without waiting for him to act, she began to tear at his uniform.

"Okay, hold on—" He tried to catch up with her. "Hold on, Tiger—"

"Don't call me Tiger. I'm not one of your kids."

"I can see that," he murmured with a trace of humor.

"Damn it, I want you." She took hold of his sex.

A short while later, they lay naked and wrung out on the bed.

When he didn't speak for the next several minutes, Jessie thought he'd drifted to sleep. She stared into the shadows, knowing the night ahead would be difficult. She'd be fortunate if sleep came to her at all.

How ironic that her escape had only brought her full circle, facing the prospect of a life without Wayne.

"When do you leave on tour?" he asked.

His voice startled her in the darkness. "I didn't know you were awake."

"You thought I could sleep after what just happened?"

"I don't know what you mean."

"Jessie, you're strung as tight as your guitar strings. I'm not sure you even knew who I was when we made love. I'm not sure it mattered."

She sighed. "I leave Monday of next week." She omitted the fact that her first gig was at Zack's Place.

"So—for now—this is our last weekend. How long will you be gone?"

"This time? Two months."

"And then?"

"I haven't found out from Todd. I don't know how far ahead he's booked me."

Propping himself on an elbow, he combed her hair with his fingers, spreading it out so that it lay like a halo around her face.

"So this is the end."

Her chest tightened painfully. She took a rasping breath. "The end of what?"

He said, "Of this small period of happiness."

"Yes." Her breath shuddered out.

"I realize I don't have the right to ask you not to go," he said.

"No, you don't."

"And you realize I want the right to demand it."

"Yes."

"And that I really can't see any solution to our dilemma."

"Don't say that." She put her fingers over his mouth.

Removing them gently, he asked, "Do you think it would be better if we made this ending final?"

"No, please." Pulling her hand from his, she caressed his face with trembling fingers. His brows, his lips, the ridge of his nose. "Please, don't. Don't ask me to."

"What are we to do? It will only get more difficult. We can only go forward. We can't go back."

"Please—" She had to stop him. She was afraid of what was coming.

He continued inexorably. "Both of us want this relationship to last. But more and more our lives will drive us apart. You know what I want. I haven't made any secret about it."

Shaking her head, she wouldn't listen. "You said—you said the first morning it was no use to talk about it."

"But the talking has to come—sooner or later."

"It can't come yet," she cried out. "We—we may say things we can't take back."

"Oh, Jessie," he said. He sighed, cradling her face. "Sweet, beautiful Jessie. You are beautiful, you know, even when you try to disguise it. Your beauty goes straight through to your heart."

Staring up into his face, she held her breath, not knowing where he was going with his gentle praise.

"I don't want to talk," he said. "I don't want to lose you. You are the most wonderful thing that's ever come into my life."

"Then don't," she said, throwing her arms around him, holding on tight to him. "We can say things to each other without speaking."

Because she was frightened, because he was helpless not to comfort her, because he was no more ready than she to face the consequences of their coupling, he took her into his arms and they began to make love.

Their bodies could be honest. Their bodies spoke to each other. Their bodies said everything their lips couldn't.

Yet the next morning when he walked her up the stairs to her apartment, they both knew their peaceful interlude was finished.

They both knew this was probably the beginning of the end.

CHAPTER TWELVE

"I HAVEN'T BEEN UP this early since I started pulling nights four years ago," Lenny grumbled.

It was Sunday morning, and he'd just arrived in Crystal Creek for a conference with Wayne and his deputies.

"You're the one who asked to be in on our visit to Zack," Gilbert reminded him.

"Just trying to be helpful. Zack's met me and knows who I am, which means that together we can scare the bejesus out of him." Lenny squinted his eyes and shadowed them with his hand, pointing skyward from the courthouse steps where Wayne and Gilbert had met him. "Is that golden orb the sun?"

"It has been too long," Gilbert said with a shake of his head. "Sorry, it's too late now to crawl back in your coffin."

"I vant to drienk your coffee," Lenny said with a certain dramatic flair.

"It'll probably kill you to ingest a cup that hasn't aged five hours," Wayne said.

Lenny turned to him, a humorous light in his eyes. "Is that why you left big-city police life? Because you liked fresh coffee?"

"Among other reasons," Wayne said with amusement.

Lenny turned around slowly and flung out his hands. "What is so special about this podunk town?"

"Smile when you say that," Gilbert instructed darkly.

Lenny ignored him. "It isn't even quaint looking."

"We leave quaint to Fredericksburg and Wimberley," Wayne said. "We keep it plain and simple in Crystal Creek."

"Don't try to explain the place to him, boss. Lenny's too jaded to understand the joys of clean living."

"Thank God," Lenny said in reverential tones.

Once inside, Wayne introduced Lenny to Roy and Bobby, and the men settled around Wayne's desk with freshly brewed coffee and two dozen doughnuts from the Longhorn Coffee Shop. Lenny laid out the new information he'd received.

"We've got a definite link between Boozer and the video piracy business. Seems a few years ago when audiotape sales started to slow down, Boozer's organization got into copying sporting events. Super Bowls, Title fights, NBA championships, that kind of thing. Once they got production going, pirating movies was a natural progression."

"How are they getting the master tapes?" Wayne asked.

"They had someone on their payroll in a distribution company, headquartered in L.A. LAPD gathered enough evidence to arrest the guy and he's plea-bargained and agreed to tell all. The L.A. cops I've talked to say they're beginning to think this is the biggest operation they've ever uncovered. Apparently, Boozer's tapes are selling by the thousands in Japan and Korea. Copyright laws in the Far East are different from ours."

"Does anyone in L.A. have a lead on where the tapes are being copied?"

"No. They were on the trail several months ago, then it went cold. They think we've caught up with it here in Texas. It'd be like Boozer to parcel out his operation. No one's ever said the guy was dumb. You know—" Lenny looked Wayne in the eye. "If you hadn't recognized Boozer and Kipling that day at Zack's, this piracy investigation would be going nowhere. Zack must love you."

"The feeling's mutual," Gilbert said under his breath.

"We still need to solidify the Texas connection," Wayne reminded everyone. "Have we found a link between Boozer and Southwestern Bar and Billiard?"

"Boozer's back in Las Vegas, but he left Kipling behind in Dallas. Dallas police are tailing him. As soon as they have something, they'll call us," Lenny said.

Wayne looked his way sharply. "Will they wait to move in until we can coordinate the effort?"

Lenny nodded. "They've agreed to wait for instructions. In the meantime, I like your idea of trying to flush Zack out. I'll let you do the talking and say my piece when you cue me."

"Agreed. Gilbert, did you contact Carmen?"

"Yes, and she understands that she and her sister are to get out of the way as soon as we appear."

"Good." Wayne glanced at his watch. "It's time to move."

ZACK HAD JUST UNLOCKED the dance hall for the cleaning women when the Sheriff and his deputies pulled up and penned in his Bronco.

He stumbled back a few steps at the show of strength. For a moment, he must have thought about running, because he looked like a rabbit searching for its hole. Next his eyes alighted on the two women. But if he'd had an idea to use them, it died with the realization that they'd hurried round behind Wayne and the others.

Some instinctive sanity apparently kicked in, since Zack neither ran nor sought to gain a dangerous advantage. Instead, he puffed out his chest and waited for the men to approach him. His face was fearful, but his eyes were hot with hostility.

"Frisk him," Wayne said.

"Hey, get your hands off me," Zack protested.

"I'm afraid it's a necessary precaution," Wayne said.

He nodded to his deputies, and Roy and Bobby proceeded to check Zack for weapons.

No one else spoke during these first tense moments.

That left Zack unable to control his jitters. "So—what's going down, Sheriff? Haven't you got anything better to do than hassle me?" Then he recognized Lenny, and his mouth flopped open.

"Howdy, Zack," Lenny said. "It's been a while."

"What're you doing here?" Zack asked.

"We've got a warrant to search this building," Wayne said. "Austin PD is just as interested in it as we are."

"You can't—"

"Oh, yes, we can. It says so right here." Wayne showed him the warrant. "We're looking for video equipment."

Zack couldn't disguise the panic in his eyes. "V-video equipment? I don't know what you're talking about. Why would we need it?"

"Good question," Gilbert said.

"W-we don't video the acts that come here. Not unless they want us to."

"We're not worried about you taping acts without their permission," Wayne said. "We have reason to believe you're pirating movies."

Zack swallowed hard. "That's crazy!" he croaked.

"We don't think so. You've been associating with suspected felons who've been implicated in video piracy."

"Who—" Zack cleared his throat "—who would that be?"

"Don't you know?" Wayne asked softly.

"Are you still harping on Boozer and Kipling?" Zack blurted out.

Wayne smiled with grim satisfaction. "I'm glad to see you remember their names."

"I—I don't mean . . . listen, they're just two guys I met. Okay, I admit I'm into them for some money. But that doesn't mean—" Zack stopped abruptly.

"Go on," Wayne suggested.

"Yeah, you'd like that, wouldn't you?" Zack's resentment flared for a second. "You'd like to see me gone from Claro County for good. Especially since Jessie's turned into your regular honey. What're you going to do? Turn in your star and follow her from gig to gig? How long do you think she'll want you without that pretty badge?"

Wayne managed to restrain himself.

Gilbert, however, had had enough. "You'll leave Ms. Reynolds out of this, if you know what's good for you."

Zack scowled at Gilbert before apparently remembering something. In the space of a heartbeat, his temper died. "I'm not saying another word until I consult my lawyer."

"Fine. Roy, Bobby, get started." Wayne motioned for them to enter the building.

"Hey! You can't do this. I tell you, I'm calling my lawyer."

"Go right ahead," Wayne said. "There's nothing your lawyer can do about a warrant, however."

"I'm going to sue, you hear? Sue you for slander! My good name's important to me. I'm a businessman—"

Wayne cut through the bluster. "Tell me about your Wimberley land."

He might as well have shot Zack from the reaction he got.

Zack's mouth opened and closed like the gills on a dying catfish. When he finally spoke, his voice was barely above a rasp. "What Wimberley land? I don't own any land."

"But you did," Wayne said, "until three or four months ago. You sold it to an outfit named Southwestern Bar and Billiard. We're having a little trouble tracking them down. You think you can help us?"

Rubbing his hands along his jeans, Zack tried to appear unfazed by the question. "I don't think so. I never met—"

"Surely someone met with you to inspect the acreage. Maybe the realtor would know how to reach them."

"I—I didn't use a realtor."

"How did this company know your land was for sale?"

Beads of sweat had popped out on Zack's forehead. He was beginning to look like a deer caught in headlights. "I uh, I...I ran an ad in the newspaper."

"Which newspaper?"

"The, uh—the Dallas one."

"Why Dallas? Why not Austin or Houston? They're closer."

"I don't know—"

"You'd have been more apt to find a buyer."

"I found one, anyway."

"What dates did you run the ad?"

Zack shrugged. "I don't know. What difference does it make?"

"Do you have a receipt for the ad space?"

"Why would I keep it?"

Wayne smiled very gently. "Because you're a businessman, Zack, who keeps track of expenses."

He turned to Gilbert. "Instruct Roy and Bobby to search for an ad receipt from a Dallas newspaper, say, from April or May. Also remind them to keep an eye out for any records or deeds on the Wimberley property, and this place as well. Tell them to take all the time they need."

Nodding, Gilbert swung around to go inside.

"Wait a minute, Gilbert." Wayne looked Zack's way. "You want these ladies to begin cleaning?"

"Yeah, yeah, I don't care. Now that you've already put on a show for them. Don't think I'll forget that, either."

"If you'll escort them in, Gilbert?"

Gilbert took the women into the building.

Now only Zack, Wayne and Lenny stood in the dusty circle created by the vehicles. By this time, sweat had darkened the underarms of Zack's shirt. His complexion had turned a dull gray, and one eyelid was twitching.

"Is there anything you'd like to tell us?" Wayne asked.

"I'm not saying nothing without my lawyer."

"Be sure and tell him I said you don't get many more chances. Does he, Lenny?"

"Not from where I stand," Lenny said. "You know, Zack, this investigation covers a wide territory. The Far East, California, Nevada, Texas. A lot of cops in a lot of places would like to break it open. You've managed to move into the big leagues, good buddy."

"I—I'm not into anything," Zack said with a desperate bravado. "I just own a bar and gamble a little."

Lenny shook his head. "I wouldn't say that. Looks to me like you're gambling your entire future." Turning to Wayne, Lenny suggested, "Why don't we go inside and let the gentleman call his attorney?"

Yet when they'd trooped into the cool of the bar, Zack refused to make a call while they were in the building. Instead, sullen and fidgety, he sat at the table with Wayne and Lenny while they listened to the sounds of the women's cleaning.

The two cops were content to let the silence build.

After a half hour or so, Bobby entered the bar from the back hallway, looking pleased with himself.

"Finished?" Wayne asked, suspecting Bobby had discovered something and wanting the tension to stretch Zack tighter.

"Yes," Bobby said.

"Find anything interesting?"

"Sure did. There wasn't any receipt or property records, but we discovered these." He handed two checkbooks to Wayne.

Wayne riffled through the books before checking more slowly. "Ahhh—these checks are the kind that make their own carbons. Hmm, that's odd."

He handed the checkbooks to Lenny before leaning over the table so that his shadow covered Zack.

"I saw three checks," he said, "for five thousand dollars each. That's fifteen thousand dollars to Southwestern Bar and Billiards. One's dated May, one June and one July. Why are you paying them? I'd have thought they'd be paying you for the land you sold them."

"They—I bought some pool tables from them. Some other equipment."

"Where is it?"

"I didn't like it so I sent it back."

"When?"

"Th-the other night. They brought a truck and hauled it off."

"That load didn't include any VCRs, did it?"

Zack's face turned ugly. "What's Tiny told you? Anything he said is a flat-out lie."

Wayne sighed heavily. "No, you're the one who's lying, Zack. You haven't been straight with us from the very beginning. You're in a lot of trouble, and only we can help you. Have Boozer or Kipling threatened you?"

Zack scowled.

"If so," Wayne said, "you'd be smart to come clean. They're not nice to people who screw up their assignments."

Zack's complexion darkened. "I didn't screw—" He stopped himself in time.

Pointing his finger toward Wayne, Zack said through gritted teeth, "You're the one who's threatening me, Sheriff. But it won't do any good. Now get out, dammit, and take your deputies with you. You haven't got anything you can pin on me. You're just fishing."

Wayne held up the checkbooks. "I'd say we landed a catch."

BY THE TIME Sunday services had ended, Gilbert and Wayne were back in the office. Lenny had left for Austin with his report of the morning visit, after suggesting the next visit they paid to Zack should be done at a civilized hour.

Bobby was off for the rest of the day. Roy was tailing Zack. The highway patrol had been notified to keep a watch on the Wimberley property. And Wayne had called Tiny to warn him about what Zack knew.

When Wayne explained some of what the lawmen were looking for and Zack's volatile reaction, Tiny decided he'd start looking for a new job that day.

IT WAS ALMOST an hour later when Gilbert came into Wayne's office. Wayne could see his deputy had something on his mind as well as in his hand.

"I didn't have a chance to tell you earlier," Gilbert said. "You got a call from Mr. Skinner yesterday. He wanted you to know Mike was doing well."

"Good."

"He also expressed his thanks that you kept his son from firing the gun. Once Michael was in treatment, he told them the whole story. Apparently it's hairier than the one you fed us."

Wayne nodded noncommittally.

"Anyway, Mr. Skinner said to tell you he realizes you probably saved Mike's life."

Gilbert paused, obviously waiting to see if Wayne wanted to continue this discussion. When Wayne said nothing, Gilbert went on to the next subject.

"I've also been authorized to give you this." He handed Wayne a framed certificate, complete with elaborate calligraphy and an embossed gold seal depicting two rifles with the symbol ∅ across them and an olive branch beneath.

The certificate read:

> To our beloved Wayne Jackson, sheriff of Claro County, for bravery above and beyond the call of duty. This certificate is presented in gratitude for the vital role you played in ending the Dawkins/Thompson Feud, and with the understanding that negotiating a treaty with a room full of peevish kinfolk requires as much courage as facing a firing squad at dawn.

It was signed by many of the town's prominent citizens, including Dr. Nate Purdy, J. T. McKinney and the Reverend Blake.

When Wayne took it and read it, he broke into laughter. "I hope Martin got one of these as well," he said.

"Oh, yes. Although he claims you should have most of the credit. I personally think the most brilliant move you made was pointing out to Cal how many insurance policies the Thompsons represented. Last time I heard, he'd already sold them six."

Gilbert offered his hand. "Congratulations, boss."

"Thank you, deputy." Wayne took Gilbert's hand and shook it.

Gilbert started to leave, then turned back around, his expression sober. "By the way, are you going to see Jessie this weekend?"

Wayne's face smoothed out into an enigmatic mask. "Why do you ask?"

"I don't like the way Zack talks about her. He worries me. He's just crazy enough to do something he shouldn't."

"He worries me, too. But as long as Roy's on his tail, he can't get into too much mischief. Besides, Jessie's leaving Austin to go on tour."

Gilbert's expression registered Wayne's curt announcement. "Oh. Well—you still might want to tell her to keep an eye out for him."

"Zack's one of the subjects Jessie and I don't talk about," Wayne said. "But you're right. I'd better see what I can do."

THINGS WEREN'T going well in the studio session. Jessie knew it, but she couldn't seem to do anything about it.

Up to now, Patrick had been extraordinarily patient, but she realized she was wasting his valuable time. He could have been working with someone who knew what they were doing.

"Stop. Desist." His voice came through her headset. When she turned around, he'd pulled off his headset, was coming out of the booth in her direction.

"What's going on?" he asked.

"I don't know." She fiddled with her pick. "I'm having trouble getting around these songs."

"This is our last real chance to work on them before you leave, Jess. I thought you wanted these arrangements to take with you."

"I do."

Patrick held up his hands in a gesture of frustration. "It's been hard to finish up with you out of town the past three Mondays."

"We may not have to worry about that in the future."

Patrick's expression immediately changed from one of frustration to conjecture. "That's not what I meant. What are you saying?"

"Wayne and I might not be seeing each other when I get back."

"Did he break it off?"

"No."

"Did you?"

"No."

"Then what's going on?"

Jessie stared at the wall, unable to meet Patrick's look. "I'm not the woman Wayne wants."

Patrick snorted with amusement. "Tell me another one. He can barely keep his zipper closed whenever he's around you."

Jessie's face reddened. "Don't be crude."

"I'm just calling it like I see it."

"What I mean is, he doesn't want to be involved with the life I lead."

"I don't blame him," Patrick said flatly. "I wouldn't be in this business if I didn't love making music. There are too many hassles and too many crazies and not enough mental health to fill up a beer can. That's why I never went into the performance end of it. I like having a life of my own with sanity included."

"I want a life of my own, too, Patrick." Jessie blinked back tears.

"Does Wayne love you?"

"He's never said it."

"Do you love him?"

"Yes." Biting her lip, she paused before saying, "But I can't change him."

"You wouldn't want to, would you?"

"Not really."

"Well—isn't he willing to give a little, too?"

"I couldn't ask it of him. His first wife didn't want children. She didn't want a home. She didn't appreciate the life Wayne had to offer. He deserves the best."

"Hey, Jess—you're not chopped liver." Patrick turned her head so that she faced him. "Any man would be damned lucky for you to love him. Have you told him?"

She shook her head. "I didn't want to add extra strings."

Something more than annoyance crossed Patrick's features. "Well, that's just great. Is that the way you've gone about pursuing your career? Have you given in, given up and walked away from it?''

"Of course not.''

"Isn't Wayne just as important?''

"I think so.''

"Then don't let him get away. You deserve the best, too. Most of the performers I work with, this is their whole life. This is all they know and all they want to know. If they're sleeping with someone, it's job related.''

"That's not fair.''

"But it's true more often than not. Relationships are fine as long as they don't get in the way. That's why one-night-stands are popular. Screw a fan and get a groupie.''

"No, I simply don't believe that's the way it has to be.''

"It doesn't have to be that way. But it is, usually. I'll tell you something, Jess. Some of these characters have the maturity of three-year-olds. When I think about them having children, I shudder. When I think of you having a child and loving it, tears come to my eyes.''

"Oh, Patrick . . .''

"You deserve to have someone to love,'' he said, "who doesn't give a damn how many CDs you've sold.''

"You there, Jessie?'' Todd called down the hall.

"Speak of the devil—'' Patrick muttered.

"I'm in here," she yelled to cover up Patrick's comment.

"Hot damn!" Todd bustled in. "Just the person I'm looking for. I've got great news, babe. I mean really great news."

"What is going on?" she asked.

"You and I are going to London town."

She sunk into the nearest chair. "London?"

"London, Dublin, Munich, Milan. They love you, babe. They love you in Europe. You're authentic country western, and they can't get enough of that."

"What? How—? When did all this happen?"

"Your CD's flying out of the record stores all over England. You're sold out in Munich."

"But I didn't know—"

"I've been working with a buddy of mine in London. I was waiting to tell you until it was a done deal."

"But—" Jessie wanted to tell him something, but she wasn't sure what.

"See," Todd said, his face settling into mulish lines, "I'm working for you all the time. I know what some people—" his eyes cut to Patrick "—are saying. That I'm not enough agent for a talent like yours. But see—I came through when it really mattered."

"But what about the national tour?"

"I'm working on that too. You know the song Clyde Miller recorded. Well, the single's headed toward platinum. He's so happy with it, he wants to see what else you've got. And—he wants to know if you'll be his opening act this spring when he tours nationally. I'm telling you, Jessie, this is the break we needed."

Then why did Jessie suddenly feel so very very cold?

"I seem to be interrupting." Wayne's voice trickled down Jessie's spine.

She twisted around to find him at the door watching them with a somber expression.

Wondering how much he'd heard, Jessie searched for something to say.

Todd was too pleased or oblivious to care about Wayne's mood. "You're just in time to hear the good news, Sheriff Jackson. Jessie's booked for three months in Europe. Well, almost booked. We have to work out the details."

"Is that true, Jessie?"

"I haven't agreed to anything."

"But signing a contract is just a formality," Todd said. "My buddy can guarantee at least fifteen gigs."

Wayne's look never left Jessie's face. "When will you be leaving?"

"As soon as she comes back from this minitour," Todd informed him, "we'll record the material she's been working on. Then we'll be taking off over the wide Atlantic. Ohhh, I like the way that sounds."

"Shut up, Todd," Jessie said. "Wayne—please listen."

"I'm listening," he said quietly. "Do you have anything to say to me?"

She shook her head helplessly. "Not now. We'll leave and go back to the apartment."

"I can't." He looked remote. "I shouldn't have come here."

"Don't say that."

"I mean," he said, with care and deliberation, "that I shouldn't have taken the time off to drive into Austin. I'm involved with a case that's going to break any minute."

He turned to leave, then seemed to remember something. "I came to tell you to look out for Zack. He's involved with this case, and things don't look good for him. He's liable to blow up. I don't want you to be around if he does. Okay?"

Her eyes brilliant with unshed tears, she nodded in wordless agreement.

CHAPTER THIRTEEN

FROM EVERY CORNER of Zack's Place applause swept over Jessie. Pointing Al's way she generated another round of cheers. Zack's patrons seemed particularly enthusiastic now that she had a local connection.

Although her performances tonight and Wednesday had been unheralded, news of her appearance must have gotten out because the dance hall was more than half full.

A few people were missing. Tiny, most particularly. When she'd asked about him, Tom, the bartender, had refused to answer her questions. Tiny's absence had been her most disappointing discovery. She'd counted on him to lend her a feeling of safety.

There was no evidence of Wayne, either. But then she'd worked hard to bring that about.

She'd persuaded Zack to leave her name off his radio ads and the outside marquee until Thursday; he apparently bought her argument that these first few sets with Al were little more than rehearsals.

Jessie hoped that by the time Wayne heard of her performing, on Friday or Saturday, she could show him that this was just an ordinary gig.

They hadn't talked since yesterday's scene. She'd almost called several times, once at three in the morning.

Remembering his stark "Do you have anything to say to me?" always stopped her. Tonight she'd sung with only part of her heart.

Apparently, however, Zack's patrons hadn't noticed anything lacking, and their warmth and approval flowed over her like a healing balm.

Acknowledging the clapping and whistling, Jessie threw Al a kiss and finally made her way offstage. One more performance and the night would be over. Four more nights, and she'd be free of Zack.

Thinking back to happier times, she was sorry it had to end this way. She'd loved appearing at Zack's Place. She'd always received a warm welcome, even during the early years when she'd been as green as grass.

This afternoon, when Zack met with her briefly, he'd been edgy and impatient. He'd barely contained his malice toward her, as if he, just as she, could barely wait for their contract to end.

Tonight she hadn't seen him at all. She wasn't sure he was still in the building, which was just as well, because she'd felt an aura of danger surrounding him.

Remembering this, and Wayne's words of warning, she hurried into her dressing room. Once inside, she turned the bolt and sagged down in the lumpy upholstered chair. She looked at the dingy walls and scarred furniture. She might as well get used to this kind of cramped cubicle. She'd be seeing a variety of them in the next several months.

Jessie mentally pulled herself up short. During this past week she'd been giving herself lectures about the upcoming minitour. She'd decided she was going to work to recapture the thrill and sense of accomplishment she'd felt early on when she'd traveled from gig to gig. When she'd discovered that it was up to her to win an audience over. When she'd first realized she had the intensity and talent and, yes, the charisma to capture an audience and hold it in the palm of her hand.

What would the audiences be like in Europe? Immediately, Wayne's reaction to the European tour filled her mind.

No. She wasn't going to think about him or their differences. Or about how his entrance into her life had affected her dreams and her future.

Right now she had a job to do, and she'd concentrate on that.

She took a deep breath to steady herself—at least as deep a breath as the gold sequined dress permitted her. It was soaked with sweat. She decided to change into the jade-green gown for the final set.

Unzipping the back and side of the damp costume, she slipped it off. She thought about removing her combination waist cincher and garter belt, but knew if she did she might be too tired to put it on again. Instead, she slipped on a silk kimono over her slip and stockings.

Settling in front of the mirror, she began to touch up her makeup. Her hair could use some work, too, she thought, studying herself critically. Lately, she'd been considering a softer look, maybe a little less flamboyant. Perhaps her costumes could be longer and flowing.

A slight breeze clued her that someone else was in the room. When she turned, she found Zack standing between her and the door. He locked it behind him.

The look on his face chilled her to the bone.

"Is EVERYONE SET to go?" Wayne asked as they pulled onto the shoulder of the road and switched off the headlights.

Lenny craned his neck around. "Yes. Everyone's in place. They're waiting for you to give the word."

"I'm glad Boozer showed up back in Dallas," Wayne said.

"So we could nab them both in Texas?" Lenny asked.

"Yeah. I talked to my friend Harry."

"And?"

"He'd have liked to do the honors, especially on Boozer. But he'll make do with raiding the Las Vegas operation."

"We may actually succeed in putting these hoods out of business."

"That's what we're paid for."

Wayne and Lenny looked at each other and shared a grim smile.

The two men were parked across the highway from Zack's Place. Gilbert and Bobby had nudged their car in behind the trees on the other side. A unit of the highway patrol had pulled up to the side of them. Roy was parked in the brush in an unmarked car, where he'd been most of the day.

This was the night. The case had broken open. Panicked, Zack had made a flurry of calls, including one to the address of Southwestern Bar and Billiard. By following those calls through various transfers, Dallas PD had made a connection between Boozer and the dummy company and were set to move in.

A Department of Public Safety helicopter had flown over the Wimberley property, and two large portable buildings had been sighted, complete with generators.

Earlier this evening, Kipling had hired a truck and with two of his men seemed to be headed toward the central Texas town. The general consensus was he would try to cart away the VCRs and tapes, if that was where they were stored. A unit of state police was on hand to arrest him when he did so.

All that was needed was Wayne's go-ahead. Since his was the only squad working around a crowd of civilians, he'd been voted to set the operation in motion. The stress of waiting was thick in the air.

Wayne picked up his mike and called Roy on the radio. "Has Zack made any moves?"

"Not for the past several hours," Roy said. "He's had some visitors."

"Anybody we know?"

"No one I've ever seen before."

"Are you still in there?"

"No."

"Then we'll sort them out later. What about Tiny?" Wayne asked.

"I haven't seen hide nor hair of him."

"He must have quit or been fired. And the bartender?"

"He's here."

"Good. I have a feeling that by the time we get through with him, he'll be ready to talk."

"How much longer do we sit here?" Roy asked.

"I thought we'd wait until the last set was over," Wayne said. "Let the place clear out." He frowned. "Considering it's Tuesday evening, there's a pack of people here."

"You should have expected that."

"What do you mean?"

There was a brief silence from Roy. "Don't you know who's performing tonight?" he asked after a moment.

"No. And I'm not in the mood for guessing games."

"Hell!" Roy's voice was heavy with distress. "And all this time I thought you knew."

"How did you get in?" Jessie asked, willing her voice to be steady.

Zack held up a key. "I own the place. Remember?" He laughed at a private joke. "Or I did, anyway."

"Why are you here? I didn't invite you." Trying not to call attention to her state of undress, Jessie pulled the kimono tighter and tied the sash.

Zack's eyes were glittering as he watched her every move. "I thought you'd know why I'm here." His voice was slurred with either drink or excitement.

Jessie fought her fear, trying to stay calm.

"I *don't* know, Zack," she said. "But I'm getting really tired of this. Say what you want to say and leave."

"Yeah, sure." Zack laughed shortly. "You expect me to obey you like a puppy?"

"Zack, remember the agreement you made with Todd."

"I don't really care about my agreement—not anymore. Your boyfriend's done his best to screw up my life, but I'm a step ahead of him. Today I sold this place for cash. I had a buyer in reserve just in case I needed him." Zack's face grew ugly. "I didn't get half of what it's worth. But at least, I'm getting out of here—" his eyes were hot as they raked her "—just as soon as I've settled accounts."

"There's no point telling me this," she said. "I have nothing to do with Wayne's work."

"Tell me another one." He moved closer to where she sat.

She stood up immediately and edged away. "Zack, I mean it. This is between you and Wayne."

"That's not how I remember it, honey. For five years that bastard didn't know I was alive. I wanted to make friends, but he wasn't having any. Then he catches me putting the make on you, and he's on me like mustard. I haven't been able to shake him since he got into your pants."

The image he evoked seemed to stir his lust. His breath grew labored. He rubbed his hands along the front of his slacks.

"Zack—" Her eyes skittered around the room searching for a weapon. "Don't do anything you'll regret later."

He laughed again. "The only thing I regret," he said, "is not screwing you years ago when you were still an easy lay."

There were many angry words she could have hurled at him, but now wasn't the time for them. Besides, she needed a clear head instead of one filled with confusion and denial.

She moved to one side, gauging the distance to the door.

He grinned. "Go ahead. Try to get around me." He held up his hands and beckoned her with his fingers. "Come on and fight me. I like it better if I have to play rough."

When he stepped toward her, she was forced backward. She realized he was close to cornering her against the wall.

A part of her knew it would be dangerous to fight him. But the thought of him on top of her produced a visceral reaction. She realized she had no choice but to make a break for it.

When she tried to dash around him, however, he grabbed her kimono. With a single yank, he tore it away.

"Oh, sweetheart—" his leer scalded her "—you are one hot bitch. I can hardly wait to get some of your hot sweet honey."

She shivered involuntarily and backed away.

Her calves hit the upholstered chair and she fell into its depths.

Looming over her, he reached down and ripped away her slip. When he tried to tear her panties, her instincts took over and she kicked and clawed at his face. He fell on her, trying to reduce her resistance, all the time fumbling with his zipper.

When she kneed his groin, he cursed and slapped her hard.

She began screaming.

"That won't do any good," he mumbled thickly, heaving with exertion. "Nobody can hear you. Besides, if you don't stop, I'm liable to use this."

He reached around his back and pulled out a pistol, which he'd apparently stuffed under his belt. Relishing the fear in her eyes, he pointed it at her temple. A rictus of a smile was smeared across his lips. "See how smart I am? I brought insurance."

Her screams turned into gulps of air.

Placing the gun on the floor by the chair, he said, "I don't want it to get in the way. Just remember I have it."

As Zack spoke, she stared up into his features. There was no trace of the man she'd once known and liked. All that remained of him was a crazed animal.

"YOU MEAN Jessie's in Zack's?" Wayne asked tautly.

"Yes," Roy said.

"Then let's get moving." Without another word, Wayne whipped the car across the highway, into the parking lot and around to the back.

Trusting Wayne's instincts, Lenny instructed everyone to proceed as planned at the front and side entrances. Then he alerted Alberta to set in motion the other coordinated efforts.

As Lenny and Wayne approached the back, laughter and music drifted out to them. A faint scream overrode the muted din.

The exit was locked. Wayne pounded on it. When no one answered, he sent his shoulder through the door.

They heard the scream again and rushed in its direction, calling Jessie's name and opening doors as they went.

The cry for help came from a locked room at the end of the corridor.

"Sheriff's Department! Open up," Wayne shouted.

WAYNE'S VOICE through the door hit Zack like a lightning bolt. When he reached for the gun, Jessie kicked him hard in the gut.

He reeled backward but managed to take the gun with him. For a moment, Jessie thought he'd try to shoot her. Then she saw the hatred on his face as he aimed toward the door.

"Wayne!" Jessie screamed. "He's got a gun! He's going to shoot you!" She reached for Zack's legs, trying to unbalance him.

Wayne kicked in the door as a bullet ripped through it. A streak of blood appeared along his side. Another shot rang out, but it was aimed wildly, since Wayne had already thrown himself into the room. He caught Zack's wrist and sent the gun flying. When it hit a wall and fell to the floor, Lenny confiscated it.

Wayne kneed Zack in the groin, and the man let out a squeal of pain. Next Wayne aimed a flurry of blows into Zack's soft middle. When Zack sagged against him, Wayne threw him up against the wall, put his hands around Zack's throat and squeezed.

"Wayne!" Jessie yelled. "Wayne—stop! Please. You'll kill him."

She stood and grabbed Wayne's arms, tugging at them as hard as she could. "Wayne..."

"Son of a bitch—deserves to die." He spoke in spurts of rage.

"I know," she said. "But I don't want you to kill him. Wayne, please—"

Her pleading finally restored his reason. He eased his hold on Zack and let him ooze to the floor.

Immediately, Jessie wrapped her arms around Wayne. "You could have been killed," she said, sobbing.

Lenny and Wayne's looks met over her head.

"I'll take out the trash," Lenny said, hauling Zack up, cuffing him and leading him away.

"I'm okay. He didn't hit me," Wayne murmured. "Jessie, are you hurt? Did he hurt you?" He tried to pull away so he could examine her.

"No. Please. Don't let me go." The words came out in shudders. "Don't you understand? I watched him pull the trigger, and I knew you were there."

The remembrance brought on tears. Wayne was still holding her when Gilbert found them.

"Heard there was some excitement—" At Jessie's state of undress, Gilbert averted his eyes.

"Hand me that robe," Wayne ordered, and draped the torn kimono around her. "Can you take care of the formalities? I'm driving Jessie home. We'll get a statement from her later."

"Sure."

After Gilbert had left them, Wayne tucked Jessie's arms into the kimono, keeping her cushioned against his body.

"Did he rape you?" Wayne asked quietly, as he reached for her purse. "Because if he did, we need to take you to the hospital."

"No. You came in time."

"Thank God."

"But how did you know—?"

"We were here to arrest Zack on that case I mentioned."

"And you had to come to my rescue instead. I almost got you killed." New tears seeped from beneath her lashes.

"Now enough of that," he said, gently chiding. "Come on, let's go home."

Leading her to the car, he tucked her in like fine china and drove her to his house. All the while she tried to control her tremblings.

It was only after he carried her inside and turned on the light that he saw her bruised cheek.

He let out a string of soft curses.

"What?" Jessie asked, wide-eyed.

"He hit you."

Her hand tentatively touched the sensitive area. "Only once." She managed to smile.

"You're going to the hospital."

"No. Wayne, please. Nothing's broken."

"If I'd known he'd hit you—" he cradled her face tenderly "—I'd have broken his face and snapped every bone in his hand."

"Shhh..." Jessie raised a hand to cover his mouth and noticed her palm was bloodstained. Staring at it, she gasped, "He shot you. You're bleeding."

She stepped back and saw the torn, bloodied shirt. "Wayne, oh my God."

"It's nothing. He nicked me. See?" He shrugged his shirt off to expose an ugly streak across his ribs.

Turning chalk-white, Jessie slumped into a chair. "He could have killed you," she whispered. "I told you to get back."

He bent down in front of her. "I couldn't do that, Jessie. I couldn't leave you with him. Besides, when you told me he was aiming for me, I knew you weren't in imminent danger. I had Lenny as backup. It was a calculated risk."

A risk Wayne had been willing to accept, Jessie realized. He'd have taken a bullet or anything else that stood between him and her. She leaned her head over her knees, feeling faint at the thought.

In a flash, Wayne scooped her into his arms and took her into the bedroom, where he laid her on the bed with infinite care.

"Wait," she said weakly, "I need to bandage you."

"You need to rest," he corrected her. "Let me get you out of these things."

Smoothing away the kimono, he undid her stockings and waist cincher. When he saw her torn panties, he closed his eyes briefly.

"If I'd seen these—" he slipped the panties off as if he could barely stand to handle them "—I really might have killed him."

Taking care not to hurt her cheek, he slipped one of his T-shirts over her head.

She laid her hand along his face. "Don't think about him anymore. He isn't worth it."

Crossing his arms over his chest, Wayne gazed at her broodingly. "Well, this settles it. You're not going on any damned tour."

Jessie tensed. A sense of foreboding nudged at her exhaustion.

"What do you mean?"

"Just that," he spoke forcefully. "You're not leaving Crystal Creek."

"Wayne—"

"Hear me out. The last time we talked, I didn't feel I had the right to say that. Now I do."

"Why?"

"Because I love you. I want to commit myself to caring for you."

Why didn't his declaration ease her doubts?

"Just like that?" she asked, her voice light but shaky.

"Oh, Jessie. I've been fighting this thing between us for weeks. Tonight when I heard you screaming, when I knew you were in danger, I admitted at last how much you meant to me."

He sank down on the bed and took her into his arms. "I love you so much. I want to take care of you the rest of our lives."

"Oh, Wayne..." She slipped her arms around his neck. "I love you, too. I knew the night of the last baseball game. Just watching you with the boys made me want to cry."

"You are everything I want." He kissed her eyes, her forehead. He sent a line of delicate kisses along her reddened cheek. "I mean for us to make a life together. But first we have to cancel this goddamned tour. Give me Todd's number. I don't want to wait until tomorrow."

As Wayne reached for the phone beside the bed, Jessie stopped him.

"Not yet," she said. "Wayne—let's talk."

He sat up, not quite facing her, his expression already closing in on itself.

"Look at me, please."

He did as she asked.

She studied his face. "Are you worried about my safety?" she asked.

He looked at her as if she were slightly stupid. "What do you think?"

"Don't be. What happened tonight was different."

"What happened tonight was typical in a business that glorifies sex, drugs and violence."

"Wayne, that's not fair. The songs I sing don't glorify any of those things. Besides," she reminded him gently, "Zack came into my dressing room because of you."

She saw defensive anger cloud his expression.

"Don't be upset," she pleaded. "I'm not telling you this to blame you, but so you'll understand. Zack hated you for what you'd done to him. It was just a way for him to settle accounts. That's exactly how he put it. So see, you can't generalize."

"I can generalize about what being on the road is like. It's dangerous and sleazy. I don't want you mixed up with it."

"I have contractual obligations."

"Like the one with Zack?"

"Wayne—"

"I told you he was dangerous. Why wouldn't you believe me?"

"I did. I just couldn't—"

"I knew how close Zack was to the edge. How much he hated me. I was going to arrest him."

"You're right," she said. "I should have listened." She couldn't help adding, "Although I'd have understood more if you'd been more honest."

His expression flared at the implied accusation. Moving off the bed, he extended the distance between them. "I was honest. But I couldn't divulge the specifics of a case. You should have trusted me more."

The word *trust* hit her hard. "How could I trust you when I didn't understand your motives?"

"Motives? What do you mean?"

At his harsh tone, she scrambled off the bed. "I knew you resented my singing."

"That's not true—except—perhaps at the beginning. I accept your music and what it means to you."

"Accept? That's a lame way of putting it."

"I appreciate your talent. I've already told you that."

"You just don't want me to develop it. You don't want anyone else to enjoy it. You want me to tuck it away except for every other Friday."

A muscle twitched in his jaw. "I've never said that."

"Then why don't you want me to tour?"

He took hold of her shoulders and said a little desperately, "Don't you understand? When you're away from me I can't protect you."

Her expression softened. "Most of the time, you won't need to."

"Most of the time. Except for tonight."

She twisted out of his hold. "I've already told you—"

"Do you think I don't know what's out there waiting for you? Drunks and loners. Honky-tonks filled with wannabe studs. Cheap motel rooms without any security."

"Wayne, I've been traveling for ten years. I'm a grown woman. I know how to take care of myself."

"I don't agree. When you're onstage, you invite men's fantasies. You're a danger to yourself."

"Are you implying for one second that I invited Zack's attack?"

"No, dammit. I'm saying that with your looks and moves, you're vulnerable to men like Zack who have sick cravings."

"And you're vulnerable to a person like Zack with homicidal tendencies. Twice, in a month, you've almost been shot."

"We weren't talking about me."

"Maybe we should. You don't like what I do—"

"I don't like parts of what you do."

"I don't like parts of what you do, either. You shouldn't have put yourself in the position you did. I'd rather have been raped than watch you die." Even as she said the words, she knew she meant them. That deep inside her was rage at the risk he'd taken.

"Now that's a stupid statement if I ever heard one," he said furiously. "There's no cause for you to be a martyr."

"Me a martyr? You've got the wrong person. You've been acting like one for the past three weeks."

He started to protest, but she interrupted him. "You've known I had contract obligations. That there were moves I had to make to further my career. Tonight," she added, "just gave you an excuse to do what you've wanted to do for some time."

"And what is that?"

"Issue an ultimatum."

"That's ridiculous."

"Either I give up the tour or I give up you."

"Jessie, I love you. I want to take care of you."

"The two aren't necessarily the same. I think you love a person I can't be."

"Jessie—"

"You have a dream of what you want. I don't fit it."

"I love you, not some dream."

"But you wish you'd never met me."

His hesitation was slight, but they both felt it.

"That's a damn lie," he sputtered, but it was too late. "You're putting words in my mouth. Why are you doing it?"

"I'm not. You're the one—"

"Maybe you're the one who wishes you'd never met me."

Her hitch of breath was slight, but they both heard it.

"Maybe," he said, his scrutiny hot and intense, "you're the one who's so wrapped up in yourself and your songs that you don't have anything left for love and commitment. Maybe there's not enough in you to offer a husband and family."

She flinched as if he'd hit her and stepped back against the door. "That's the cruelest thing you've ever said to me," she whispered hoarsely.

The veins stood out on his neck. His face was dark with color. Yet his voice was even as he reminded her, "No more cruel than what you've said to me."

She went to the window to stare out of it sightlessly. "This is why we didn't talk before. Because we held all these words inside us. And loving each other isn't enough." Turning to face him, she blinked away tears.

"I don't know. Is it?" he asked. "I love you. I want you to be in my life. All I ask is that you're not in and out of it. I can't have an on-again, off-again, long-distance marriage."

"And I can't put my career on hold because of your demands."

A long silence put more distance between them until Wayne groaned painfully.

"Oh, Jessie, don't let's do this to each other. Come to me." He held out his arms. "We're tired. We're not making good sense. Let's get some sleep before we discuss this any further."

There was nothing she wanted to do more than escape into his embrace. There was comfort in his arms, but she knew it was illusory.

And the things they'd said had been all too accurate and logical. They were only putting off the inevitable.

She shook her head. "I can't. Tomorrow's finally here. We can't hide our differences any longer. We've known from the beginning that we only had a little time."

Wayne let out a particularly savage string of expletives.

She picked up her kimono and shrugged it on. "I'll go to the kitchen and call Nora to come get me. Tomorrow, I'll give Lenny my statement in Austin."

The phone call took Jessie less than a minute. Back in the living room, she paused to study Wayne intently, as though she wanted his image to remain vivid in her mind. Then she carefully picked up her purse.

Her hand on the doorknob, she said, "I love you. Goodbye."

CHAPTER FOURTEEN

"HAVE YOU SEEN Wayne since Tuesday night?" Patrick asked Jessie the next Sunday morning, as he watched her pack her bags for the gig in El Paso.

"No. There wasn't any point in it. Besides, you know how busy I've been working at the studio."

Patrick refused to be sidetracked. "Why isn't there any point in it?" he asked.

"The things we said were inevitable. We'd been ignoring our differences all along." The ache inside her belied her stoic tone.

"So—you had a fight. So what? Aren't lovers entitled to more than one argument?"

She slumped on her bed and set her suitcase to wobbling precariously. "There are just too many things working against us."

"Idiocy, for example?"

She heard the depth of Patrick's frustration.

"Please, don't fuss at me," she pleaded, "or tell me what I should or shouldn't have done."

"Somebody has to. Jessie, be honest with me. Do you really want to take off for El Paso today?"

"Not entirely." When she felt her lip trembling, she steadied it with her teeth. "But I plan to make this road trip a successful one. If I start breaking contracts or performing halfheartedly, my career will go down the tubes. And I won't let that happen."

"Does Wayne understand how you feel? Did either of you think to discuss things rationally?"

"It wasn't a very rational night."

"Which makes me wonder why you chose it to discuss your future."

"Neither of us," she confessed, "has much experience in these matters."

"Do you love him?"

"Yes. But I'm not sure that makes a difference."

"Doesn't it? I won't say Wayne's the only man for you, Jessie. That's a cliché. I'll just say the odds of your finding someone more suited are about a zillion to one, give or take a few million."

"That's just it. We don't match at all."

"How?" Patrick asked. "And I don't mean careerwise. When you're together do you get along?"

"Yes. He's an intelligent, kind, funny man."

"How's your love life?"

Jessie flushed. "Better than average."

"Do you enjoy the same things?"

She nodded and smiled. "We laugh together. He has this rumbly chuckle—"

Patrick held out his hand. "You don't need to explain."

"He's gentle," Jessie said, remembering Wayne with the Little Leaguers. "He's so big and strong. Yet he keeps his power contained."

"You're probably the only woman who's broken through his granite exterior."

"Probably," she admitted.

"And he's probably the first man who's meant more to you than a song."

"That's true."

"Well . . ."

"Well what?"

"You've just made my case. You're perfect for each other. The Sheriff and the Singer. Catchy title for a song."

"Are you going anywhere with this?" Jessie said, half amused, half perturbed.

"If you let him go—"

"I know, I know, I'll always regret it. That's a cliché too."

"But it's true."

Turning her back to him, she was suddenly absorbed in her packing.

"Fine," Patrick said resignedly. "Don't listen to me. Listen to the voice inside yourself. You remember what it's like on the road. The soggy, greasy meals, the long hours of driving. You know performing won't give you all the satisfaction it used to. You know you can't pour all your emotions into your songs anymore. It won't work. You can't go back."

When he saw her wiping her eyes, he knelt in front of her. "I'm sorry. But I had to say this."

"I know, I know. It's for my own good."

Reacting to her tears, Patrick sat beside her on the bed and threw his arm over her shoulders. "Oh, Jessie—I wish I could say something more helpful."

She knew he meant well. But all she could think about was Wayne's arms around her.

She jumped from the bed, throwing Patrick off balance. "I just remembered—I have to run my schedule down to Mrs. Peters. I—I'll just be a minute."

Patrick was left to stare after her, wondering what else he could have done to help.

"WE MANAGED to shut down the Los Angeles pipeline and the Las Vegas headquarters," Wayne said, as he gazed out over Eugene's porch railing. "And we have Boozer and Kipling on a long list of charges."

"And Zack?" Eugene asked, idly petting Cleo.

"He's being held in jail without bond." On attempted rape and attempted murder among other charges. But Wayne didn't feel he needed to elaborate.

"How on earth did a penny-ante gambler like Zack get involved in a multimillion-dollar pirating operation?"

"Because he didn't stick to penny-ante bets. By this spring he was into Boozer for close to two hundred thousand dollars. He confessed everything to Gilbert." Wayne didn't mention that he hadn't trusted himself to be in the same room with Zack.

"They must have seen him coming a mile away." Eugene shook his head sadly. "A chicken ready for the plucking."

"Yeah. Once he'd run up his tab, they put the squeeze on him to work for them. After he'd set up the operation, it was too late to get out."

"And you're telling me they were copying tapes in the back rooms of Zack's Place."

"That's what I'm telling you."

"Right here in Claro County. Amazing. I could almost feel sorry for Zack," Eugene said, "if I hadn't heard what he tried with your Ms. Reynolds. Heard you rode up on your white charger to save her. Heard you actually got nicked this time."

He eyed Wayne quizzically, but couldn't get a rise. Seeing that, Eugene went back to the original subject. "And I guess Zack sold them the Wimberley land."

This time Wayne responded, "Zack used it as collateral early on. Later they had the idea to set it up for storage if they had to stash the equipment."

"You know," Eugene said, "we've had enough excitement around here to last a lifetime. What with the Gordon Jones business and now this?"

Wayne let his gaze drift down the river. "I guess that means I can expect peace and quiet for the next several years."

"It depends."

"On what?"

"On whether you settle down and straighten out your love life."

Wayne scowled. "Now look—I came by to satisfy your curiosity and fill you in on everything that's happened."

"Not everything."

"This is a courtesy visit."

Eugene chuckled. "You know I ain't got no couth, much less any courtesy."

Wayne snorted. "I know you're a nosy old man with too much time on your hands."

Eugene laughed harder. "That's God's own truth. I'm driving my wife crazy. That's why she's always glad to see you."

"Well, I'm not here to provide you with any more diversion. My business is my business, no matter what you and the town think."

"Hmmm—you sound a mite tetchy. Been getting enough sleep?"

Casting Eugene a dark look, Wayne knew better than to say anything.

Besides, it was time to leave.

But, instead of getting up and saying goodbye, Wayne pushed the toe of his boot against the wooden flooring, setting his chair to rocking once more.

"You know, Wayne—you and Roy are kind of like sons to me."

Wayne was surprised at the serious tone and unusual use of his given name. He wondered what was coming.

"Oh, I know Roy's a little set in his ways," Eugene went on. "But he's loyal and honest."

"I couldn't do without him. He's great on routine."

"I've never thanked you adequately for keeping him on."

"Eugene, you know I wouldn't have fired Roy just because he's not a real go-getter. I'm not that shortsighted."

"Then why did you and Jessie break up?"

"What does Roy have to do with Jessie?" Wayne asked, bewildered.

"You were pretty damned shortsighted to let her go."

"I didn't let her go. It just wasn't working."

"Why?"

"Because we don't fit into each other's life." Wayne realized he was close to shouting only after he'd finished.

Eugene didn't bat an eye at Wayne's tone of voice. He just waited for Wayne to finish before saying, "That's not how this love business works, you know. Of course, you don't fit into each other's life. What you do is, you create a new one between you."

"That's easy enough to say."

"And damned hard to pull off. A lot of couples don't even try. That's why there're so many split-ups. People turn tail and run at the first sign of trouble."

"Is that what you're saying we did?"

"Did you?"

"We didn't have a chance to try. Time ran out on us."

Eugene looked puzzled.

"Jessie'll be out of town for the next several months. There's no telling where that bastard's booked her."

"Is she gone now?"

"I think so. I asked her not to go."

"Why?"

"Because...it's dangerous for her. I wanted to take care of her. I didn't want her to have to put up with the likes of Zack. She'd just suffered a traumatic experience. I thought touring would be too hard for her."

"As hard as breaking up with you?"

"Just when," Wayne asked irritably, "did you get to be Ann Landers?"

"Hey—if you don't want to talk about this, that's fine with me."

When Wayne glanced at Eugene warily, he looked the soul of sincerity.

"I just figured—" Eugene shrugged "—that you could use someone standing back a ways."

After Eugene swatted a fly Cleo was intent on catching, he settled back in his rocker as if he meant to doze.

"Well, I guess I'll be going." Wayne remained seated.

"Always glad to see you, son," Eugene said lazily.

Both men continued to rock, causing the boards of the porch to squeak out a rhythmic refrain.

"Have you ever seen her, Eugene?" Wayne asked, surprising himself.

"Nope. Just heard about her."

"She's absolutely beautiful."

"That's what I hear."

"And talented."

"I've heard that."

"And all I have to give her is me and Crystal Creek."

"Does she love you?"

"She said she did."

"Then I'd let her decide if you and Crystal Creek are worth investing in. Seems to me, you and this town could be sort of a haven. To insulate her from the crazies in the business."

"It's the business I hate," Wayne said bitterly. "But I can't ask Jessie to leave it. That's not fair to her."

"No, it's not. Do you love her?"

"Yes." He remembered her stinging words in regard to his loving, and an awful realization came over him. He propped his elbows on his knees and put his face in his hands. "The truth is—she's right— I don't want to share her."

"I don't blame you."

"But that's not love, is it?" He faced Eugene. "That's ownership."

"You're learning."

A troubling thought came Wayne's way. "What if she's had time to think things over and realizes I've been a selfish bastard from the very beginning?"

"I wouldn't try to deny it when you see her," Eugene counseled. "I certainly wouldn't leave her long to brood," he went on. "She might find out she can do without you."

"Hell, she's done without me for twenty-eight years."

"And you've done without her even longer. But once you find the right person, being alone's like a prison sentence."

Reaching over, Eugene took hold of Wayne's shoulder with his gnarled fingers. "You're not gonna find someone better, son. Playing the lotto of life, you lucked into a jackpot."

"I don't play lotto. I'm not a gambling man."

"Everyone's a gambler when the stakes are high enough. Are they this time?"

"Yes," Wayne said.

BUT FATE CONSPIRED against any reunion with Jessie. Wayne had tried calling her several times the first week, but she'd obviously already gone since all he got was her answering machine.

He'd be damned if he'd try to make up with an electronic gadget. He'd have to wait until he could see her face-to-face.

Wayne's office was swamped, however, with follow-up paperwork to the Great Tuesday Raid. He drove up to Dallas at one point to untangle a legal snag and spent four days in Las Vegas at a preliminary hearing.

Harry and Charlene put him up at their place, and they had a good visit. But he knew both of them suspected something was wrong. He had a feeling they'd spoken to Bobby to get the particulars he wasn't ready to reveal.

Then, as was so often the case, a rash of petty crimes demanded his attention. Three weeks passed before he was able to take time off and leave Gilbert in charge.

During those weeks he lost a lot of sleep in aching wakefulness, and spent hours in soul-searching reverie.

Sometimes his yearning for Jessie grew so strong, it cramped his stomach. He'd reach for her at night and awaken in despair.

Memories of her shook him unbearably. Her hair tumbling over her guitar as she strummed the strings. Her look of concentration while she searched for a melody. The essential innocence intensifying her sensuality.

The old shorts and shirts she wore to conceal her charms. Her passion and tenderness. Her ease with others. He missed her onstage and offstage and in his arms.

For the first time, he was certain that he wanted her back. All of her. Unconditionally. Without reservations.

She was the best thing that had ever come into his life.

He hadn't fallen in love with little bits of her, the parts that were convenient. He'd fallen in love with Jessica Reynolds, complete and indivisible. The musician and the lover, the performer and the small-town girl. Loving all of her meant accepting all of her.

Loving her meant—and this was the part he'd wrestled with—helping her become all that she could. And that meant supporting her in her career.

He threw away the mental blueprint he'd made of his future. Jessie and he would simply design a new one.

DRIVING into Austin on a hot September morning, Wayne knew where he was headed. He'd be an unexpected visitor, which was exactly how he wanted it.

Sure enough, Todd turned a little green when Wayne walked into his office unannounced.

"Listen—" Todd pointed to the cordless phone at his ear "—I'm on long distance."

"I can wait," Wayne said, selecting a chair.

"It's kind of private," Todd said pointedly.

"Then I guess you'd better end it." Wayne knew he was being unreasonable, but just then he didn't care.

Todd mumbled something and ended the call. "So how's the famous sheriff?" he asked in an attempt at sarcasm. "I've been seeing you on TV."

Wayne shrugged. "In another week or so I'll be old news."

"Yeah. Sounds like you skewered good ol' Zack like a shish kebab."

Standing to his full height, Wayne towered over Todd's desk. "Good ol' Zack attempted to rape Jessie at gunpoint. Did you know that?"

Shaking his head, Todd blinked and swallowed hard.

"I told you Zack was dangerous," Wayne went on. "I warned Jessie not to appear there. You talked her into it."

"Hey, man—" Todd threw up his hands "—I was just doing my job."

Wayne smiled grimly. "We'll have plenty of time later to talk about your job. Right now I want the locations and dates of Jessie's appearances on this road trip."

"Didn't she give them to you?" Todd's question held malice.

"No. That's why I'm here."

Todd shrugged. "Then she must not want you to know where she is. And as her agent, I have to abide by her wishes."

"Did she say she didn't want me to know?"

"N-no," Todd admitted.

"Then give me the list." Wayne leaned over the desk until he was square in Todd's face.

Todd was frightened, Wayne could tell, but his mouth was set mulishly.

"You can threaten me all you want," he muttered. "I'm not handing it over. Why should I?" His voice grew incensed. "You've already caused enough trouble. You're the reason she's not going to Europe."

Wayne straightened in surprise.

"Biggest thing I've done for her in years," Todd complained, "and she refused it. Don't think I don't know it was because of you."

Wayne was so preoccupied by Todd's revelation that he barely noticed what the other man was saying.

"How am I supposed to handle her—" Todd elaborated his grievances "—when she won't take what I can get? I'll be glad when you're finally out of her system."

"If I have anything to do with it," Wayne said, "you can forget about that. I think you should know I'm in Jessie's life for good. So I guess you and I had better learn to live with each other."

Todd's face crumbled into horror.

Wayne couldn't help a chuckle as he left the agent behind.

PATRICK WAS at the studio when Wayne caught up with him thirty minutes later. After they exchanged brief greetings, Patrick waited for Wayne to explain his visit.

"I've just been by Todd's office," Wayne said, "and he won't tell me where Jessie is."

"I'm not surprised," Patrick said. "He sees destiny slipping through his fingers."

"Can you help me?"

Shaking his head, Patrick said, "I sure can't. I know she was booked in El Paso, then Midland. But those gigs only lasted a couple of weeks. You might check with Jessie's landlady."

"I've met her."

"Jessie always gives Mrs. Peters a copy of her itinerary."

"Thanks. I'll go see her." He eyed Patrick thoughtfully. "If I need a reference with Mrs. Peters, can I use your name?"

"That depends." Patrick's words were a challenge, and both men knew it. "Are you going after Jessie?"

"Yes." Wayne didn't elaborate.

"You've hurt her."

"I know."

"It's been hard on her—your not knowing what you wanted."

"I'm sure about what I want now," Wayne said.

"I got a letter from her last week. I don't think she's doing well."

"I'll be good for her in the future. You have my word on it."

"You need to know—" Patrick searched Wayne's features "—that Jessie's music means a lot to her. If you cut her off from it, she'll suffer."

"I don't intend to do that." Wayne wanted to be honest with Patrick. "I'd like to help her with her music. If you'll help me learn how."

"It's a deal," Patrick said, holding out his hand.

Wayne took it, and they solemnly shook on the agreement.

But Patrick wasn't finished. "You also need to know that what you've seen of Jessie's career is just the beginning. There's a lot of hype in this business, but I'm telling you, Jackson—with or without Todd she's headed for the top."

Patrick paused, still studying Wayne's expression. "Are you ready to put up with a famous wife trailing legions of adoring fans? You're a very private man."

"I'm also a determined one. I'll insist on some privacy for us both. Besides—" Wayne grinned "—in Crystal Creek she won't be Jessica Reynolds, the famous singer, so much as just Jessie, the sheriff's wife."

Patrick's face showed both amusement and vast relief. He let out a long whistle. "I sure am glad to hear you say that," he confided.

"Oh, yeah?" Wayne lifted a brow.

"If you hadn't assured me you were going to treat Jessie the way she deserves, I'd've had no choice but to tear right into you." He looked Wayne over from his five-foot-ten vantage point. "I can tell you here and now that just thinking about us tangling depressed me a bunch."

"I only beat people senseless every other Tuesday," Wayne said straight-faced.

Patrick grinned. "I hear Zack has a few scars. I hope you gave him one for me."

THE VISIT with Mrs. Peters was positively cozy. The first thing she offered him was coffee and fresh cinnamon rolls.

Wayne didn't need a reference from Patrick. Mrs. Peters beamed when she realized she might be playing Cupid.

"I've been saying to myself for a long time now that Jessie was too nice a girl to stay single." Her words flustered her. "Not that I mean—I'm sure—"

"I plan to marry her," Wayne said.

"Oh, I'm so glad." Mrs. Peters breathed a sigh. "I hope you don't think I'm gossiping."

"Of course not," Wayne said diplomatically.

"I figured," she confided, "that it wouldn't be long before some clever young man snatched Jessie up."

"I don't know how clever I've been, but I do intend to grab her."

Mrs. Peters flushed happily with his declaration of intent.

While she went to find the itinerary, Wayne sipped his coffee musingly. Everyone except Todd seemed to feel Wayne was right for Jessie. Now all he had to do was convince her of that.

Waving the paper before her, Mrs. Peters hurried back into the room.

When she handed it to Wayne, he couldn't wait to study it.

Running his finger down the page, he saw that Jessie was appearing at the Driftwood Saloon in Oklahoma City.

Oklahoma City was a good ten hours from Austin straight up Interstate 35. He could take a plane, but he bet there wasn't a flight until tomorrow morning. Besides, he needed his truck at the other end of the line.

He glanced at his watch. It was just two o'clock, which meant he'd pull into the Driftwood Saloon sometime after midnight. Not for a moment did he consider finding a motel in, say, Dallas, to break the tedium of the journey. Not now that he had Jessie located.

He must have frowned because Mrs. Peters patted his shoulder. "Don't you worry, Sheriff Jackson. I'm sure when you see her, she'll listen to you."

"Thanks for your confidence. I hope it's not misplaced."

"You will invite me to the wedding?" she asked a little wistfully.

"Just as soon as we set the date," Wayne said.

JESSIE GLANCED at the travel clock she kept on her dressing room vanity. It was two o'clock. She was due to rehearse in another thirty minutes. Fortunately, she'd worked with the band before. They were good musicians, they liked her new songs and they'd been quick to master Patrick's arrangements. For several of the numbers she worked alone.

Picking up her guitar, she played a sequence of chords and warmed up her voice. Tonight, she'd be performing a new song, the song she'd worked on endlessly. The song she played to bring Wayne near.

She'd never felt farther away from him than today. Somehow leaving Texas had emphasized the distance between them. A distance that wasn't measured in miles alone.

Yet these past dreary weeks had been good for something. They'd taught her valuable lessons. Lessons she hadn't wanted to face before.

She'd learned about loneliness. A cold weary loneliness that withered her spirit.

She'd learned about loss. The loss of a man's love and all the love inside herself.

She'd learned about need. The need to commit to someone, to climb out of her skin.

Most of all she'd learned that without Wayne the music died.

Her choices were clear. She knew what she wanted. She just wasn't sure she could convince Wayne she meant it.

When she'd canceled the European tour, Todd had been furious. But she couldn't see Wayne again with such a barrier between them. Besides, the thought of being an ocean away from Crystal Creek at this point in her life was more than she could bear.

She would see Wayne—at least once more. Her one certainty was that she must see him. In person. Face-to-face. No phone calls or letters. She had to be able to use all her powers of persuasion.

She'd never been so scared or so exhilarated at the prospect.

But for tonight she'd have to be content with playing his song.

CHAPTER FIFTEEN

SHE WAS FIRE—blazing fire—and shimmering darkness.

Wayne let out a ragged sigh as an overwhelming need pulsed through him. He sagged against the wall, hoping the players clustered around the pinball machines and video games hadn't noticed his body's reaction.

It was after one in the morning, he'd been driving eleven hours, and he could, he supposed, blame his response on fatigue. But he knew better. It was Jessie's singing that stirred him. Purely and simply she possessed his soul.

Even with a wall separating them, with the buzz of customers and electronic noises intruding, he still felt as if he'd been kicked in the gut. If anything, the intimate knowledge he had of her only intensified the exquisite frustration. He had to fight the urge to stride into the other room and show her he was there.

But he didn't want to distract her before she'd finished the last set. He knew she had a sixth sense about his presence. He also was aware he stood out in a crowd.

So all he could do was prop himself against the wall next to the entrance to the dance hall and let her music reach out to him. Just as on that first night at Zack's Place, he didn't have to watch her to feel the impact.

Even without looking he could have detailed her features. The cloud of fiery hair. The flawless complexion. The jade-green eyes that were gateways to her soul. The dainty nose, the stubborn chin. The sensual lips caressing the music. The full lush body that was his to adore.

For the first time since he'd arrived, he could ignore the seediness of the saloon, its dimly lit bar, the ramshackle hall devoted to musical entertainment, the garish gadgetry of the video arcade.

As Jessie sang, it was easy to imagine just the two of them without the late-night ragtag crowd intruding.

He recognized almost all of her material. She performed several cuts from her current album. He also heard songs she'd been working on with Patrick. The torch song she'd performed at Zack's Place had the male customers caterwauling, and Wayne realized ruefully that his hands were balled into fists.

There was a slight pause when she finished one of her familiar ballads. He felt the hesitation and sensed a snag in her composure. When she spoke he detected raw emotion in her voice.

"For my last selection of the evening," she said, "I want to sing a song I've been working on awhile.

I didn't know when I started exactly where it was headed. But I've learned a lot about myself the past few months, and once I understood my feelings, the rest came easy."

Despite her words, it sounded as if it was hard for her to speak.

"There's a special someone in my life," she continued, "and I wish more than anything he was with me tonight. If y'all don't mind, I'll pretend he's listening. I want to dedicate this song to the man I love."

Wayne's chest felt heavy. He rubbed his palm along it as he anticipated her first notes. The quiet from the other room signaled the audience also waited, sensing this song was very special to the singer.

For a few moments, she strummed her guitar, providing a foretaste of the haunting melody. Then alone, in the circle of a single spotlight, she began to sing the initial verse:

I planned my tomorrows.
I thought that I could,
I didn't understand
What it was to lose.
I didn't understand that
I couldn't choose.
Grief doesn't seek favors
Or ask when or who.

After a still silence she riffed a minor chord and began the refrain with a throb in her voice.

I could live without you for the rest of my life,
I could do without laughter and a child's sweet
　　smile.
And forget the silken feel of a loving sigh,
And cry bitter tears until the tears ran dry.
Oh, I could live without you till the day I die,
But it wouldn't be living if you asked me to try.

I hadn't planned on your coming.
I thought I could choose
Who I let in my life,
Who I gave my love to.
Love isn't right
It can only be true.
Love wasn't what we asked for,
But we couldn't refuse.

I could live without you for the rest of my life,
I could do without sunshine and a child's sweet
　　smile.
And forgo the silken touch of a lover's sigh
And cry lonely tears until the tears ran dry.
Oh, I could live without you until the day I die,
But it wouldn't be living if you asked me to try.

Now we must ask
Will there be you and me?
I know I need you,
But I can't make you need me.

I want you beside me.
But you have to choose.
Please, remember as you're choosing
All the love we have to lose.

I could live without you for the rest of my life,
I could do without rainbows and a babe's dear
   cry.
And forget the silken sound of my love's sweet
   sigh
And weep endless tears until the tears ran dry.
Oh, I could live without you till the day I die,
But please . . . please, don't ask me to try.

There was a moment of silence as the notes faded, before a wave of applause swept the hall. Wayne knew if he could see Jessie, he'd find that she was crying.

He wiped his hand across his face and discovered there were tears in his eyes.

JESSIE COULDN'T have spoken if she'd tried. Fortunately the audience didn't need an end to the performance. They realized the song provided its own climax. She left the stage and the clapping slowly died away.

The entire time she'd performed, she'd had that eerie feeling only Wayne could provoke. She'd searched the room, knowing he couldn't possibly be present. Yet—when she'd sung his song, he'd seemed as close as her heart.

Without that sense of closeness, the wave of lone-liness that struck her on the way to the dressing room was painfully intense.

"Hey, sugar, remember me?" A figure stumbled from the shadows. "You sang so fine you just about broke my heart. Course, you break my heart into little pieces every time I hear you."

Jessie turned warily to the customer who'd been there three nights running. He was harmless, but usually tipsy by this time and hard to shake off.

"Thank you," she said and turned to escape through the doorway.

"Hey, wait a minute, sugar." He lurched toward her. "Don't go so fast." He grabbed at her hand. "I just wanted to tell you what your singin' does to me."

"I think," a deep voice said, "you've told her enough for now."

Jessie twisted around and saw Wayne herd the customer in the other direction. She was still stand-ing like a statue when he returned.

He must be a hallucination, Jessie decided. A tall rugged hunk of hallucination.

Clearing her throat, she murmured, "Rescuing me is getting to be a habit with you, mister. Is your white charger outside waiting to carry us into the sunset?"

"Will a rusted-out pickup truck do instead?"

"Yes—oh, yes!" She launched herself into his arms. "Oh . . . oh—" She realized she was crying.

"I love you," he whispered.

"I love you, too."

"Where's your dressing room?"

"Through that door. Wayne, I have so much to say to you."

"Let's grab your things and get out of here. We'll talk later." But once they were inside and alone, he took the time to kiss her until she almost fainted.

"I have things to say to you, too," he whispered against her throat. "But they'll keep till we have some privacy." Pulling away, he traced her face with his fingers. "Take off your stage makeup, Jessie. I want nothing between me and your beautiful skin."

Waiting only long enough for her to wipe her face clean of cosmetics and discard her costume for jeans and a shirt, he tucked her under his arm and headed unerringly toward the motel next door.

When he held out his palm for her key, she stared at him nonplussed.

"I got your complete itinerary from Mrs. Peters," he explained, "including where you're staying. Earlier tonight, before I went over to the Driftwood, I persuaded the woman at the desk that my intentions were honorable. The badge helped."

"I see. You really do have a way with the ladies," Jessie said.

"The only lady I want my way with is you." He hauled her inside. "Now, where were we?" Encircling her waist, he pulled her up his torso so that her lips were on a level with his.

"I wanted to tell you—" she began.

Covering her mouth with his, he said, "You already have. Besides, we have plenty of time to talk. There's no hurry."

But there was an urgency. A physical imperative that led them to the bed.

They tumbled into it, still clutching each other, managing to strip away clothing without losing their place.

"This one's going to be quick," he muttered, spreading her legs.

"Where have I heard that before?" She found it difficult to sound amused when she was gasping with pleasure.

"You'd better," he muttered, settling into her deeply, "have heard it from me."

She chuckled. "Now that you mention it...oh—ahhhhh."

Never before had she gone straight from laughter to fulfillment.

Staring up at his fiercely tender features, her mouth sagged open with delighted disbelief.

He plunged his tongue inside her and matched it to the rhythm of their coupling.

Within moments, they both climaxed.

Slowly, they came back to reality in a tangle of arms and legs.

"WAYNE," JESSIE SAID, "I'm not going to Europe."

"You will if you need to."

"But I've already told Todd."

"I know. I've talked to him. But I want you to think about it more before you make a final decision."

"Wayne, I've decided." She knelt beside him with her knees nudging his side. She wanted to be able to study his expression. "I never want to be away from you again. I want to live in Crystal Creek with you. I can write my songs there."

"And when you need to try them out, you'll hit the road."

"Only into Austin," she said with a shiver. "These past few weeks have been the worst of my life."

"For me, too. Listen, we'll work out the details later. And that includes tours. Your career is so much a part of you, Jessie. I want to help you with it."

She couldn't help gasping at the gift he was offering.

"I'll tell you how you can help," she said impulsively. "Marry me."

Without any hesitation, he promised, "Tomorrow if you want."

"Give me babies." She smoothed one of his brows.

"Four sounds good to me."

"Give me loving." She kissed him.

"Every day and night I'm with you."

"Give me more songs to sing about our life together."

"The song you sang tonight," he said, "was the most beautiful gift anyone's ever given me."

Her expression was clear as she gazed into his eyes. "Wayne—without you, the music died. If I hadn't written that song, I couldn't have written anything."

He closed his eyes for a moment and heaved a ragged sigh. An expression crossed his face that she wasn't sure she'd seen before.

"Jessie," he said, his tone rough with emotion, "I have to say this. But it's very, very difficult."

"Say it," she instructed softly.

"I've learned how to do a lot of things in my life. I've learned to do without love. I've learned how to lose people. I've learned how to grieve and then move on. I've learned that giving to others is a gift to myself. I've even learned to trust to a certain point. But you—" He faltered and tears seeped from under his lids.

Jessie knew she was seeing a Wayne no one else had ever glimpsed.

"You are the only one—" his voice cracked with the effort "—the only one who's ever been able to teach me how to need."

As he opened his eyes and gazed at her, his expression was stripped of defenses. "It's very frightening to need you so badly. I've been fighting that fear since the first day we met."

Stroking one of his muscular arms, she smiled down into his rugged features, savoring the look of him. His chocolate-brown eyes, more revealing than they'd never been before. His straight brow, his patrician nose, the carved-out cheekbones, the obstinate jaw. Lord, how she loved this man. Every inch of him.

"You are," she said softly, "the most courageous man I've ever known, Sheriff Jackson."

"But I was a coward about you." He cradled her face with his fingers. "I almost lost you because of my selfishness. My refusal to accept what was really keeping us apart. When I realized that, I was more scared than ever."

His hands smoothed down her neck to cradle her breasts. "I need you in every way, Jessica Reynolds. And I don't intend to put any conditions on our life together. Dammit," he said ferociously. "We'll make this marriage work."

She leaned into his hands, feeling deliciously secure. "I don't think it'll be all work, Sheriff Jackson."

"I think you just changed the subject." But the forays with his lips indicated he was eager to go along.

"Did you really like the song?" she asked dreamily as she draped herself over his body. "I thought I'd make it the first cut on the new album."

"Good idea. That'll be the CD that goes platinum," he forecast.

She caught her breath. "Do you believe in me that much?"

"More," he whispered, encircling her with his arms. "The world is waiting to discover the wonder of your music, Jessie." Before she could say more, he covered her lips with his.

There was a long wordless passage filled with small sounds of pleasure, before he interrupted their activities for one breathless moment. "But promise me no one but you will ever sing my song."

"I promise." She kissed him on the brows, the eyes, the lips. She even planted a kiss on his Adam's apple. "That song is just for you and me."

Relive the romance...
Harlequin and Silhouette
are proud to present

A program of collections of three complete novels by the most-requested
authors with the most-requested themes. Be sure to look for one volume each
month with three complete novels by top-name authors.

In September: **BAD BOYS**   Dixie Browning
                                        Ann Major
                                        Ginna Gray

No heart is safe when these hot-blooded hunks are in town!

In October: **DREAMSCAPE**   Jayne Ann Krentz
                                        Anne Stuart
                                        Bobby Hutchinson

Something's happening! But is it love or magic?

In December: **SOLUTION: MARRIAGE**   Debbie Macomber
                                        Annette Broadrick
                                        Heather Graham Pozzessere

Marriages in name only have a way of leading to love....

Available at your favorite retail outlet.

REQ-G2

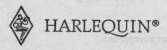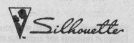

**Fifty red-blooded, white-hot, true-blue hunks
from every State in the Union!**

Look for MEN MADE IN AMERICA! Written by some
of our most poplar authors, these stories feature fifty of
the strongest, sexiest men, each from a different state in
the union!

Two titles available every other month at your favorite
retail outlet.

In November, look for:

STRAIGHT FROM THE HEART by Barbara Delinsky
(Connecticut)
AUTHOR'S CHOICE by Elizabeth August (Delaware)

In January, look for:

DREAM COME TRUE by Ann Major (Florida)
WAY OF THE WILLOW by Linda Shaw (Georgia)

You won't be able to resist MEN MADE IN AMERICA!

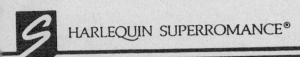
HARLEQUIN SUPERROMANCE®

1993 Keepsake

CHRISTMAS

Stories

Capture the spirit and romance of Christmas with KEEPSAKE CHRISTMAS STORIES, a collection of three stories by favorite historical authors. The perfect Christmas gift!

Don't miss these heartwarming stories, available in November wherever Harlequin books are sold:

ONCE UPON A CHRISTMAS by Curtiss Ann Matlock
A FAIRYTALE SEASON by Marianne Willman
TIDINGS OF JOY by Victoria Pade

ADD A TOUCH OF ROMANCE TO YOUR HOLIDAY SEASON WITH KEEPSAKE CHRISTMAS STORIES!

HX93

When the only time you have for yourself is...

STOLEN moments ™

Christmas is such a busy time—with shopping, decorating, writing cards, trimming trees, wrapping gifts....

When you do have a few *stolen moments* to call your own, treat yourself to a brand-new *short* novel. Relax with one of our Stocking Stuffers—or with all six!

Each STOLEN MOMENTS title
is a complete and original contemporary romance that's the perfect length for the busy woman of the nineties! Especially at Christmas...

And they make perfect **stocking stuffers**, too! (For your mother, grandmother, daughters, friends, co-workers, neighbors, aunts, cousins—all the other women in your life!)

Look for the STOLEN MOMENTS display in December

STOCKING STUFFERS:

HIS MISTRESS Carrie Alexander
DANIEL'S DECEPTION Marie DeWitt
SNOW ANGEL Isolde Evans
THE FAMILY MAN Danielle Kelly
THE LONE WOLF Ellen Rogers
MONTANA CHRISTMAS Lynn Russell

HSM2

WORLDWIDE LIBRARY

BE PART OF CRYSTAL CREEK
WITH THIS FABULOUS FREE GIFT!

The attractive Crystal Creek cowboy boot brooch—beautifully crafted and finished in a lovely silver tone—is the perfect accessory to any outfit!

As you share the passions and influence of the people of Crystal Creek ... and experience the excitement of hot Texas nights, smooth Texas charm and dangerously sexy cowboys—you need to collect only three proofs-of-purchase for the Crystal Creek cowboy boot brooch to become YOURS ... *ABSOLUTELY FREE!*

HOW TO CLAIM YOUR ATTRACTIVE CRYSTAL CREEK COWBOY BOOT BROOCH ... To receive your free gift, complete the Collector Card—located in the insert in this book—according to the directions on it. If you prefer not to use the Collector Card, or if it is missing, when you've collected three Proofs from three books, write your name and address on a blank piece of paper, place in an envelope with $1.95 (Postage and Handling) and mail to:

IN THE U.S.A.:
HARLEQUIN CRYSTAL CREEK PROMOTION
P.O. BOX 9071
BUFFALO, NY 14269-9071

IN CANADA:
HARLEQUIN CRYSTAL CREEK PROMOTION
P.O. BOX 604
FORT ERIE, ONTARIO L2A 5X3

Below you'll find a proof-of-purchase. You'll find one in the back pages of every Crystal Creek novel ... every month!

PREMIUM OFFER TERMS

Requests must be received no later than March 31, 1994. Only original proofs of purchase accepted. Limit: (1) one gift per name, family, group, organization. Cowboy boot brooch may differ slightly from photo. Please allow 6 to 8 weeks for receipt of gift. Offer good while quantities of gifts last. In the event an ordered gift is no longer available, you will receive a free, previously unpublished Harlequin book for every proof-of-purchase you have submitted with your request plus a refund of the postage and handling charge you have included. Offer good in the U.S.A. and Canada only.

Here's a proof of purchase— start collecting today!

```
   ONE
PROOF-OF-PURCHASE

   088-KAW
```
Crystal Creek

CCPOPR